## *"Are you okay?"*

She steadied herself on the wall, taking a deep breath of relief before turning around to speak to her rescuer. But the words died in her throat.

Bright blue eyes and a broad chest obstructed her view. Even on a dark Paris night those blue eyes would have attracted her attention. He was tall and dark-haired and was wearing a simple white T-shirt and jeans with a dark wool coat on top.

He smiled as he looked down at all the people below. "You could be right. I'm sorry if I startled you. But you looked frightened."

"I was. Thank you." She shook her coat free, letting some air circulate around her, and pulled her red hat from her hair. "There, that's much better."

"It certainly is." He was smiling appreciatively at her, and for a second she was unnerved. But no. There was nothing predatory about her rescuer. He had kind eyes. The man exuded sex appeal from twenty paces. If her up-close-and-personal alarm was going off it wasn't because she was scared—it was because it had been jolted back to life. About time, too.

She held out her hand toward him. "Ruby. Ruby Wetherspoon, from England."

His warm hand closed around hers. "Alex," he said simply.

Her eyes glanced up and down his body. White T-shirt, blue jeans and black boots. But the dark wool coat seemed a little strange for a young guy—a little formal.

"Are you from here?"

The corners of his lips turned upward. "Close enough."

Mystery. She liked it. Perfect for New Year's Eve.

Dear Reader,

Every girl wants to write a story about an imaginary prince and an imaginary kingdom. Writers at Harlequin actually get to do it!

I always said I wouldn't write a fictional kingdom, but the temptation was just too much. Alex is inspired by David Gandy—just in case the white trunks don't give it away—and Ruby is inspired by Rachel Bilson. I've had pictures of these two on my walls the whole time I was writing this story, and I have to admit to shedding a tear when it seemed Princess Ruby wouldn't get her happy-ever-after. Even though I'm the author, sometimes *I* don't even know how it will happen!

I love to hear from readers. Please feel free to contact me at scarlet-wilson.com.

*Scarlet*

# The Prince She Never Forgot

—

## Scarlet Wilson

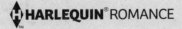
HARLEQUIN® ROMANCE

Recycling programs
for this product may
not exist in your area.

ISBN-13: 978-0-373-74323-0

The Prince She Never Forgot

First North American Publication 2015

For questions and comments about the quality of this book, please contact us at CustomerService@Harlequin.com.

**Printed in U.S.A.**

HARLEQUIN®
www.Harlequin.com

**Scarlet Wilson** wrote her first story at age eight and has never stopped. Her family have fond memories of *Shirley and the Magic Purse*, with its army of mice, all with names beginning with the letter *M*. An avid reader, Scarlet started with every Enid Blyton book, moved on to the Chalet School series and many years later found Harlequin.

She trained and worked as a nurse and health visitor, and currently works in public health. For her, finding Harlequin Romance was a match made in heaven. She is delighted to find herself among the authors she has read for many years.

Scarlet lives on the west coast of Scotland with her fiancé and their two sons.

### Books by Scarlet Wilson

#### HARLEQUIN ROMANCE

*The Heir of the Castle*
*English Girl in New York*

#### HARLEQUIN MEDICAL ROMANCE

*Christmas with the Maverick Millionaire*
*Tempted by Her Boss*
*A Mother's Secret*
*Her Firefighter Under the Mistletoe*
*An Inescapable Temptation*
*Her Christmas Eve Diamond*
*West Wing to Maternity Wing!*

##### *200 Harley Street Series*

*200 Harley Street: Girl from the Red Carpet*

##### *Rebels with a Cause Series*

*The Maverick Doctor and Miss Prim*
*About That Night...*

##### *The Most Precious Bundle of All Series*

*A Bond Between Strangers*

Visit the Author Profile page
at Harlequin.com for more titles

This book is dedicated to our newest family addition, Luca Cole Dickson. Already gorgeous, well-behaved and utterly charming, the ladies in later life won't stand a chance!

# PROLOGUE

*Ten years earlier*

SHE COULD FEEL the electricity in the air, feel the excitement. It seemed as if everyone in the world had decided to celebrate New Year's Eve in Paris.

She was jostled along with the crowd, being practically carried off her feet on the route from the Champs-élysées towards the Eiffel Tower.

'Aren't you glad you came?' her friend Polly screamed in her ear, sloshing wine over her sleeve. 'This is the best place in the world right now.'

'Yes, it is,' murmured Ruby.

It certainly beat sitting at home in her flat, brooding over the job that wasn't to be or the boyfriend who never should have been.

Polly gave a squeal. 'The fireworks will be starting in an hour. Let's try and get near the front!'

Ruby nodded as she was shouldered from behind. There were ten in their group but it was getting harder and harder to stick together. 'I need to find a bathroom before we head to the fireworks,' she whispered to Polly. 'Give me five minutes.'

There were cafés and bars open all the way along the Champs-élysées, but unfortunately for her just about every female in the city seemed to have the same idea that she had.

She waved to Polly, 'Go on without me. I'll meet you at the sign we saw earlier.'

The group had already planned their night with precision. Dinner on a riverboat. Drinks in the hotel. A walk along the Champs-élysées and rendezvous at the Eiffel Tower for the fireworks. They'd already picked the spot they planned to stand at in case anyone got lost—which on a night like tonight was a certainty.

She stood in a queue for an eternity before finally heading back out to the thronging crowds. In the thirty minutes it had taken to get access to a bathroom it seemed the whole of Paris had started to congregate in the streets.

The crowds were sweeping along the Avenue George V, carrying along anyone who happened to be standing close enough. It was one part terrifying, one part exhilarating.

The crowd was even thicker at the Rue de l'Université. The street was packed, with everyone heading directly to the base of the Eiffel Tower. Ruby glanced at her watch. Visiting the bathroom hadn't been such a good idea. There was no way she was going to be able to find her friends in this crowd.

But she wasn't too worried. The mood of the crowd was jubilant. People were drinking wine and singing. The atmosphere and heavy police presence made her feel safe—even if she was alone.

Around her she heard dozens of different accents: snatches of English, Italian and Japanese all mixed in with French. The streets were lit with multi-coloured lights and a variety of decorations and garlands left over from Christmas. She unfastened the buttons on her red wool coat. She'd expected Paris to be cold in December, but the heat from the people around her meant the temperature was rising.

She clutched tightly onto the bag strung diagonally in front of her, keeping her hand clasped over the zipper. Pickpockets were rife in Paris at New Year's. They'd all been warned to keep a close hold of their belongings.

Her phone beeped just as she was in sight of the Eiffel Tower and she struggled to move out of the thronging crowd. It had practically ground to a halt, with people from behind still pressing ahead. The streets were packed. There was no way forward.

She moved sideways, unzipping her bag and pulling out her phone.

Where are you?

It was from Polly. Her friends were obviously waiting at their designated meeting point.

She typed quickly. Not sure if I can get to you, but I'll try. She pressed Send just as someone bumped her from behind and the phone skittered from her hand.

'Oh, no!'

It was kicked one way, then another, quickly going out of sight. She tried to push her way through the crowd sideways, but that proved impossible. It was a sea of people. And she was heading in the wrong direction.

'Hey, watch out. Ouch!'

Her feet were trampled, her ribs elbowed and the wind knocked from her. It was impossible. She looked up for a few seconds, to try and make her way through the crowd, then looked down again amongst the stampeding feet, trying to track down her phone.

A thud to her shoulder sent her flying into a group of rowdy Germans.

'Sorry...sorry.'

They were laughing and joking and smelling of beer. She tried to find her way through but it was virtually impossible. There seemed to be nowhere to go.

Her chest started to tighten. They weren't doing or saying anything untoward, but the sheer amount of people meant they'd started to crowd around her, closing in. She tried to take a deep breath and lifted her elbows up, edging her way to the side. But the only place she seemed to be moving was closer and closer.

There was a waft of beer-soaked breath on her

cheek. Too close. Too invasive. A hand at her back, someone pressing against her hip.

'Let me out. Let me through. Move, please!'

A hand reached down between her shoulders, grabbing her coat and pulling her upwards. The air left her lungs momentarily and her feet were still stuck amongst the crowd. A strong arm wound around her waist and pulled her clear. Her feet stopped unsteadily on a wall at shoulder height to the throng.

'Are you okay?'

She was teetering on the wall. The hand and arm that had steadied her had pulled away the instant she was free. She reached and grabbed hold of the dark sleeve in front of her, trying to regain her balance.

The voice sounded again. 'Are you okay? Are you drunk?' There was a slight edge of disappointment to the voice.

She steadied herself on the wall, taking a deep breath of relief before turning around to speak to her rescuer. How dared he accuse her of being drunk?

But the words died in her throat. Bright blue eyes and a broad chest obstructed her view.

Even on a dark Paris night those blue eyes would have attracted her attention. He was tall, dark-haired, with a broad chest, wearing a simple white T-shirt and jeans with a dark wool coat on top. Trust her to find the best-looking guy in Paris and have no reliable witnesses. No one would believe her.

She automatically lifted her hands. 'No. No, I'm

not drunk. I just got stuck in a crowd going in the opposite direction from me.'

His demeanour changed. The skin around his eyes creased as he smiled. 'What? You're going home already? You don't want to see the fireworks?'

His accent sent tingles across her skin. He sounded French, with a little something else.

He was teasing her, and now she could actually breathe she could take a little teasing.

She sighed. 'No. I'm not going home. Not tonight anyway. Of course I want to see the fireworks.' She held out her hands to the bodies pressed below. 'Just not like this.' The crowd had ground to a halt. She stared across at the sea of people. 'I was supposed to be meeting my friends.'

'You are lost?' He sounded concerned.

'Not exactly.' She turned back to face him, getting a whiff of woody aftershave. 'We were meeting at a sign near the Eiffel Tower.' She shook her head. 'I have absolutely no chance of getting there now.'

She had no intention of leaving the safety of this wall any time soon. She only hoped his friends weren't all about to join them and there'd be no room for her to stay here.

He smiled as he looked down at all the people below. 'You could be right. I'm sorry if I startled you but you looked frightened. I thought you were beginning to panic in the crowd.'

Her heart had stopped fluttering in her chest and her breathing was settling down. It had been an odd feeling, and so not like her. Ruby Wetherspoon didn't tend to panic.

'I was. Thank you. I've never really been in a crowd like that before.

It had definitely been a bit claustrophobic.' She shook her coat free, letting some air circulate around her, and pulled her red hat from her hair.

'There—that's much better.'

'It certainly is.'

He was smiling appreciatively at her and for a second she was unnerved. But, no. There was nothing predatory about her rescuer. He had kind eyes, even if the man exuded sex appeal from twenty paces. If her up-close-and-personal alarm was going off it wasn't because she was scared—it was because it had been jolted back into life. About time too.

He nodded slowly. 'Crowds can be…difficult.'

It was an odd choice of words, but then again her hesitant French would sound much poorer than his English.

'And you'd know?' She was curious.

His face crinkled. It seemed her half-inquisitive, half-sarcastic question was lost on him.

She held out her hand towards him. 'Ruby. Ruby Wetherspoon from England.'

His warm hand closed around hers. 'Alex,' he said simply.

Her eyes glanced up and down his body. White T-shirt, blue jeans and black boots. But the dark wool coat seemed a little strange for a young guy—a little formal.

'Are you from here?'

The corners of his lips turned upwards. 'Close enough.'

Mystery. She liked it. Perfect for New Year's Eve.

Under normal circumstances she might have felt a little nervous, a little wary around a mysterious stranger. But Alex didn't give her those kind of vibes.

*Trust your instincts.* That was what her gran had always told her. And she should have. Because if she had she probably wouldn't have found her boyfriend in bed with her ex-best friend. Truth was, she couldn't wait to see the end of this stinker of a year.

She glanced around. For the moment they were the only two people perched on this precarious wall. 'Well, Alex from "close enough", where are your friends? Am I about to get trampled and thrown back to the crowd when they all want a place on this wall?'

She sent a silent prayer upwards. What was the betting they were all gorgeous and female?

He shrugged. 'I lost them too. I climbed up here to look for them. Then I decided I liked the view.'

She turned to face where he was looking. Of course. A perfect view of the Eiffel Tower. For now it had a row of white lights running up the outside of its edges. The sun had set a few hours ago and it stood out like a beacon in the dark sky.

She'd been so busy fighting her way through the crowd that she hadn't really had time to stop and take in the sight.

'Wow. I just remembered why I came here,' she breathed.

A few people shouldered past beneath them, knocking into her feet, and she wobbled again. His arm rested around her waist to steady her, and he didn't move it once she'd regained her balance.

'So, why is an English girl in Paris for New Year's Eve?'

Why, indeed? She was still asking herself that question. And Mr Gorgeous Mysterious Stranger didn't really need the whole truth. Maybe just a tiny part.

'Visiting a boyfriend?' he added.

It was a loaded question. Was he really testing to see if she was taken?

She sucked in a deep breath and tried not to let the idiot smile that was whooping and dancing around in her brain actually appear. 'My flatmate Polly persuaded me it was time to try something new. We usually spend every New Year's in London. We did try a Scottish lodge once, but that was a disaster. Snowed in with no power and no booze.'

He was laughing at her now.

She held out her hands. 'What girl would say no to Paris on New Year's? This place is just amazing...' Her voice tailed off. 'And, to be honest, I'm not sorry to see this year go.'

'You've had a bad year?'

'Somewhere between a wrecking ball and a demolition derby.'

She could almost see his brain trying to make sense of her words.

'Ahh. You sound sad. But surely not everything about this year can have been bad?'

Perfect. Her own Pollyanna.

He was right. Of course he was right. She'd just needed someone to remind her.

She gave a little nod. 'Of course not. There have been a few good things. I qualified this year.'

'As what?'

'A speech and language therapist.'

'Well, that sounds great. Congratulations.'

She nodded. 'Yeah. Yes, it is.'

Three years doing a course she'd absolutely loved. Her placements had been fabulous, letting her practice all her skills and making her realise exactly what she wanted to do.

'So why aren't you jumping for joy? You'll get to do the job that you want. Some people would give anything for that.'

His voice sounded a little wistful.

Wow. She must sound an ungrateful misery-guts. But there was something easy about talking to a perfect stranger. Someone who didn't know all the people or personalities involved. Someone completely independent.

'I should be. I know. It's just that I really, really

wanted to work in one area. I did two training stints there, but by the time I'd qualified there was only one job and they gave it to someone with more experience.' She shrugged. It still stung. She'd had her heart set on working there.

'Where was it?'

'In London. A specialist speech and language unit attached to the biggest children's hospital. I loved it there. The staff were really special and the kids... they just made my heart melt.'

'What kind of things did you do there?'

He seemed genuinely interested.

'I worked with children with specific language impairment and language disorders. Those kids made progress every day.' She held up her finger and thumb. 'Even if it was just in the tiniest way.' She smiled again, caught up in the memories. 'I even worked with children with hearing problems. Seeing the look on their faces when they got a cochlear implant and heard for the first time...' She shook her head. 'It was magical. It was exactly what I wanted to do.' She lifted her eyes to meet his. 'These things stay with you for ever.'

He was looking at her with such intensity, such sincerity, that it took her breath away. Here, in a city with over two million people, he was looking only at her.

She couldn't imagine how she'd done it, but she seemed to have completely captured his attention—just as he'd captured hers.

His voice was low and deep. 'So you don't have a job now?'

Even the timbre of his voice sent butterflies along her skin. Those two glasses of wine earlier seemed to have finally hit her system. Any minute now she was going to have to find some food before her brain was truly addled. No guy could have this kind of effect on a girl? Not in real life anyway.

She shook her head in an attempt to find some clear thoughts. 'I do. And I don't mean to sound ungrateful. I've got a job at a stroke unit, working with patients who've suffered a stroke and are having trouble with speech.'

He kept smiling at her—one minute looking serious, the next as if she amused him. Those teeth were perfect. Too perfect. He must be a model. He probably advertised toothpaste.

He raised his eyebrows. 'But that sounds just as important as the other job.'

Clear, rational thought. Easy when you didn't dream about the place where you wanted to work every night.

She cringed. 'I know. I *know*. I don't mean to sound like that. I'm lucky to have a job. Not everyone on my course got one. And once I get there I know that'll love it.' She gave a sad smile. 'It's just not what I'd hoped for, that's all.'

She heard him suck in a deep breath. 'We don't always get what we hope for, Ruby.'

His voice was serious. It made her curious.

He couldn't possibly have any idea of the kind of thoughts that were circulating in her head right now. Her imagination was running riot. Handsome mysterious Frenchman. Gorgeous, smelling good enough to eat. Polly wouldn't believe a word of this. Any minute now someone would pinch her and she'd wake up.

Time to get back to reality. Time to get a little nosey.

'So, Alex. What do *you* do? Do you work around here?'

He shook his head. 'I'm like you—just visiting for New Year. I'm in business. Boring things. Investment banking.'

*Smash*. The first dream broken. Not a model. But what interested her most was how he'd described his job. This guy gave very little away.

'Why do you do it if it's boring?'

'Because I'm expected to. It's a job.'

Another tell-nothing answer. The less he said, the more she was curious.

His phone buzzed and he pulled it from his pocket and frowned.

'Is it your friends? Are they looking for you?' She looked through the crowd, expecting to see a bunch of Amazonian blondes charging in to steal their prize back.

He shook his head. 'Nothing like that.' He stuffed the phone back in his pocket.

Ruby bent forward and peered into the crowd

below. 'I dropped my phone. It's probably smashed to smithereens.'

'Smithereens? What is that?

He wrinkled his nose. It made him even cuter, if that was humanly possible.

'You know—broken into lots and lots of tiny pieces. Irreparable.'

He nodded. 'Aha. Can't be fixed?'

She smiled. 'You got it.'

His hand tightened on her waist, edging her a little closer, and she didn't object. She liked his hand there. She was happy standing next to his shoulder with his arm anchored around her.

'So, your friends... The ones you're here with. Will they be looking for you?'

He gazed across the crowd. 'I'm quite sure they are.' He shrugged. 'But I don't always want to be found.'

Hmmm... More mystery. He was so good at deflecting questions. It was almost an art form.

He turned towards her, pulling her so they were face to face. 'Are you comfortable without *your* friends, Ruby Wetherspoon? Are you happy to watch the Paris fireworks with some strange man who pulled you from the crowd?'

It was the way he said it. The way he looked at her. The gentle smile on his face and the twinkle in his eyes. For a second she didn't want to breathe.

The wind caught her curls and blew them across his face. He laughed and took her hair in his hand, smoothing it down and tucking it behind her ear. She lifted her hand and put it on his chest. She could feel his warm skin on her palm through his thin T-shirt. She could feel the curling hairs on his chest.

The man just oozed sex appeal. If anyone had told her this time last year that she would be standing here, now, like this, she would have shaken her head in disbelief.

But right now there wasn't any place else she'd rather be. 'You're not a stranger,' she said simply. 'You're Alex.'

The countdown started around them.

*Dix...neuf...huit...sept...*

'Yes,' he murmured. 'Tonight I'm just Alex.'

The world around them exploded. Multi-coloured lights flickered up and down the outside of the Eiffel Tower. And Alex bent to kiss her.

The fireworks around her were nothing to the ones exploding in her brain. She didn't do this. She didn't do any of this. But everything about it felt right.

This was the kind of thing she could tell her grandkids about when she was an old woman. *I once kissed a gorgeous Frenchman in Paris on New Year's Eve.*

Because this *was* a fairytale. This wasn't real life.

Except Alex's kiss was more than a fairytale. It was right up there with an award-winning movie.

Tingles were going to places that tingles hadn't been in a long time. One of his hands was resting gently on her lower back—the other was holding the back of her head. Except it wasn't *holding* the back of her head…it was *caressing* the back of her head. His fingers tangled through her hair, gently moving with tantalising softness to the side of her face.

If she could capture this moment and stuff it in a jar she would keep it for ever.

His lips finally pulled free and she had to stop herself reaching out for more. When her eyes finally opened his blue gaze was on her, his fingers still on her cheek. She'd thought the moment would be gone. But it wasn't.

It was still exploding in the stars all around.

He smiled at her. People were still shouting in the street beneath their feet, jumping up and down, and a million mobile phones were being held aloft to capture the last few seconds of the firework display.

'Happy New Year,' he whispered.

'Happy New Year,' she murmured. She couldn't wipe the smile off her face. It would probably last for eternity.

They stood for a little while as the firework display came to an end and the lights on the Eiffel Tower finally finished.

He grabbed her hand in his. 'What say we get away from all this? Do you want to find something to eat? To drink?'

Her eyes flickered towards the far-off sign where she was to meet her friends. People were still tightly packed around it. There was no way she would be able to find her friends, then fight her way back through the crowd to Alex. The choice was simple.

'Food sounds good.'

The crowd around their feet had dispersed a little. The excitement of the countdown and the end of the fireworks display had sent people dispersing into the surrounding streets.

He jumped down and reached his arms up to catch her around her waist as she sat on the top of the wall, and he placed her gently on the ground.

Getting through the crowd was much easier with Alex in charge. No one seemed to argue with a broad-shouldered, six-foot-four man. He swept her along easily, pulling her behind until most of the crowd was behind them.

For a few seconds she thought there was a strange group of men behind her—all in black, with earpieces. But seconds later they'd vanished and she forgot about them.

By the time they reached Avenue George V the street was still busy but the crowd was gradually beginning to thin out. There were a number of open restaurants and cafés still serving customers. Alex hesitated a second outside of the door of the Four Seasons, then pulled her over to one of the other nearby restaurants with tables on the street.

He pulled out a chair and gestured for her to sit down. She rubbed her hands together and smiled at his good manners. It had been a while since she'd met anyone who'd pull out a chair for her.

'Are you cold? We can sit inside.' He pointed at her fingers.

'No, it's fine.' The restaurant looked claustrophobic, packed with people. It was strange, but outside seemed more private.

A waiter appeared quickly and nodded to Alex.

'What would you like, Ruby? Wine? coffee?' He picked up a menu. 'Food?'

She smiled. 'I'll have a cocktail.' Her eyes scanned the menu. 'I'll have a Royal Pink Circus—and the biggest piece of cake they've got.'

Alex grinned and reached forward and grabbed the menu. 'What *is* that? Hmm…vodka, champagne, raspberries and violet syrup. Interesting choice.'

He turned and spoke in rapid French to the waiter.

Under the warm light from the restaurant she got a clear view of the man she'd just kissed. Under dim lights he'd been gorgeous. Under street lights…*wow*.

She couldn't help but smile. No phone. No camera to record the moment. Typical. Her friends would never believe this. His blue eyes stood out even from across the table, complemented by the lightly tanned skin she hadn't noticed before and the shadow along his chin.

'So, what plans do you have?'

She shrugged. 'I don't have my phone so I can't contact my friends.' She waved her arm. 'But it's fine. I know where I am from here. I can find my way back to my hotel.'

She gestured towards the Four Seasons.

'For a second I thought you were going to take me in there.' She glanced down at her red wool coat, jeans and boots. 'Somehow I don't think I would have got inside.'

He gave a little shake of his head. 'Oh, you would have got inside.' He reached over and took her hand. 'But I wasn't talking about right now. How long are you in Paris?'

Mysterious Alex was getting better by the second. He actually wanted to know if she was staying.

'Just another two days. We go home on Friday. What about you?'

'I don't really have a fixed timetable. I can go home any time. Do you want to do some sightseeing for the next two days? See a little more of Paris before you go home?'

Her heart gave a little leap. She was here with a group of friends, but Polly wouldn't mind if she spent some time with a sexy French guy—in fact after this last year she'd probably encourage her.

She nodded as the waiter appeared. 'That sounds fun.'

He set down the raspberry cocktail in a sugar-frosted glass. She took a tiny sip. The alcohol was stronger than she'd expected and the bubbles from the champagne flew up her nose. She choked and laughed.

'Wow|! This Royal Pink Circus is a doozy!'

'What does that mean?' asked Alex as he took a sip of his beer.

'You know—extraordinary, spectacular. A doozy.'

Next came the cake. If it could even be described as that. This was no delicate *petit-four*. This was honest-to-goodness the biggest piece of cake in the universe. Seven layers of sponge, cream, raspberries and sauce.

She picked up her fork and took a bite. 'Oh, wow…' She leaned back in the chair. It had been hours since she'd had dinner. Alex was smiling at her again, with a twinkle in his eye. 'Would you like a piece? This is to die for.'

He shook his head. 'Don't let me deprive you. I'm getting enough pleasure seeing the look on your face.'

'Didn't you order anything?' She waved at the empty space in front of him, poising her fork above the cake again.

'I did, but I asked the waiter to bring your cake first.'

She swallowed another heavenly spoonful, 'I could get used to this kind of consideration, you know.'

Something flickered across his face that made her wonder if she'd made some kind of dreadful *faux pas*.

But Alex just nodded in agreement. 'And I think I could get used to Ruby Wetherspoon, who knows how to eat a piece of cake.'

She licked her fork. 'What? Do the people around you not eat?'

He lifted his eyebrows as the waiter reappeared and put a plate down in front of him, with the biggest BLT and portion of French fries she'd seen in a long time. She reached over and grabbed a fry.

'Not like you,' came his amused reply.

She shrugged. 'They certainly don't skimp on portions here. I'll need to remember this place. What's it called?' She looked at the name and screwed up her face. 'Too difficult. I'll just need to remember it's next to the fairytale hotel.'

'The fairytale hotel?' He'd started to eat and was making short work of the fries.

She nodded her head sideways. 'Yeah, next door. Isn't that the hotel every little girl wants to stay in when she comes to Paris?'

'I thought that was Cinderella's Castle at Disneyland?'

'Yeah, well. I'm older now. Tastes change.' She eyed her cocktail again. 'You know, you're going to hate me. But this is going straight to my head. Do you think I could order a coffee instead?'

He gave a wave of his hand and ordered her a coffee.

The cocktail might be a little strong, but the cake was perfect. The restaurant was perfect. The ambience in the street was perfect. And Alex...? Even more perfect.

'Have you been up the Eiffel Tower yet?' he asked.

She nodded, then leaned across the table and whispered, 'Don't tell anyone, but I thought I was going to be sick. It was okay looking into the distance, but when I looked down…' She made a swaying motion in her seat and shook her head. 'Bad idea.'

He laughed. 'And have you been to Versailles and the Louvre?'

She nodded. 'I queued for ever to see the Mona Lisa.'

He raised his eyebrows. 'What did you think?'

She wrinkled her nose. 'Honestly? Smaller than I expected—and a bit dark. But do you know the strangest thing? I still wanted to reach out and touch it.'

'She mesmerised you. Just like she did Leonardo. What about Notre Dame? Have you been there yet?'

She nodded again.

He held up his knife and fork. 'How long have you been here?'

'Just a few days. We've tried to cram in as much as possible.'

'Is there anywhere you'd still like to see?'

'Of course! This is Paris.' She counted off on her fingers, 'I still want to visit the Sacré Coeur and Montmartre—oh, and the Père Lachaise cemetery.'

He took a drink of his beer. 'So, I offer to take you sightseeing and you want to visit dead people?'

He slid down in his chair a little—he seemed to be relaxing more and more as their conversation continued.

'Well, I guess I bring out the best in you.'

She laughed. 'It's supposed to be beautiful—enchanting. Haven't you ever walked around a cemetery before? In the summer it can be so peaceful. I actually quite like wandering around and looking at the inscriptions in the gravestones. There's a few in our local church that have a skull and crossbones on them, showing that people had the plague. It's fascinating.'

His smile spread from ear to ear. 'Ruby, every time I think I might know you a little you say something else that surprises me.'

'Is that bad?'

He shook his head. 'No, it's good. *Very* good.' He reached over and took her hand. 'I'm sure I can find some things in the next two days for us to visit.'

'But today's New Year's Day. Everywhere will be closed.'

'Don't worry about that. I'll work something out.'

She was so wrapped up in him—in the way he was smiling at her, the way he was flirting with her—that she almost didn't notice the men in long black coats until they were almost on top of them.

One of them put a black-gloved hand sternly on Alex's shoulder, bent down and spoke quietly in his ear. She couldn't make out a word.

'Alex? What's wrong? Who is this?'

The expression on his face changed instantly. First it was a flare of anger, then it was a pure panic. He stood up, sending his chair flying.

'Alex?'

The black-coated man barely even acknowledged her presence.

'Ruby, I'm sorry—I have to go.' He fumbled in his coat for his phone. 'Give me your number. I'll call you.'

Her hands went automatically to her bag. No phone. She'd lost it.

'I don't have my phone, and I can't remember what my number is.'

She felt like an idiot. Everyone should know their mobile number. And she did—she had it written down at home—but right now she couldn't tell him if her life depended on it.

'What's wrong, Alex?'

He shook his head. He wasn't focused on her any more. He looked shocked.

'It's my family. Tell me where you're staying. I'll send you a message.'

She rattled off the name of the low-budget hotel where they were staying. He mumbled something to the man behind him.

'I'm sorry. I need to go. I'll send you a message later.'

He walked around to her side of the table and bent to kiss her. It was the briefest moment, but his lips came into contact with hers in the lightest of kisses. A brush like a butterfly's wings.

And then he was gone.

Surrounded by black coats, disappearing down the street.

The fairytale was over.

*January*

Ruby crashed through the door with her shopping bags, work folders and uniform over her arm.

Polly was sitting cross-legged on the sofa, eating a plate of noodles. She nodded towards the kitchen. 'Come and sit down, Ms Misery. Noodles in the pot and wine in the fridge.'

She was knackered. Honestly and truly exhausted. Between the long hours and the killer commute every day, this job was proving tougher than she'd ever thought. But today had been a winner. Today she'd finally believed that her work had helped a patient regain a little part of his speech. 'No' had been the finest word she'd heard in a while.

She poured the wine and tipped the rest of the noodles into a bowl, kicking off her shoes and thudding down sofa next to Polly. 'What are you watching?'

'Just the news. How was your day?'

She put the first spoonful of noodles into her mouth. It was like a chilli explosion. Polly had a penchant for spicy foods, and as she was the cook in the house Ruby was getting used to it. She took a few quick gulps of wine to try and quell the burn.

Her eyes flickered to the screen and she inhaled quickly, coughing and spluttering as her noodles went down the wrong way.

Polly turned and laughed, leaning over and slapping her hand on Ruby's back. 'Was the chilli kick that strong?'

But Ruby couldn't answer. Her eyes were streaming. She swallowed as best she could. 'Turn that up,' she said, pointing at the screen.

'What?' Polly mumbled, her mouth still full of food.

'Turn it up!'

She started throwing cushions and newspapers around, searching for the TV remote, which seemed to have an innate ability to hide whenever she left the house. Finally she spied it, hiding part-way under the sofa. She pointed it at the TV and pressed the volume button hard.

Polly just stared at her open-mouthed.

*'There are unconfirmed reports that King Leopold of Euronia is seriously unwell.*

*'The normally quiet principality has seen a flurry of activity in the last few days as private jets have been seen landing at the state airport. Crown Prince Alexander has returned home after a recent sojourn in the US, where he was apparently working with MIT and Harvard University.*

*'Prince Alexander, the only child of widowed*

*King Leopold, is rarely seen. He is an astute busi-
nessman who is passionate about his country. Ru-
mours have circulated in the last few years about
King Leopold's declining health and his lessening
public engagements.*

*'Crown Prince Alexander was seen returning in a
private jet in the early hours of New Year's morning,
quickly followed by dignitaries from the surrounding area. We've been told to expect a statement in
the next few minutes.'*

'It's him,' Ruby croaked, pointing at the screen.
'It's Alex.'

It was almost as if an elephant had sat on her
chest, stopping her breathing.

Polly dropped her fork and bowl on the table.
'What?' She glanced from Ruby to the TV and back
again. 'Him? *He's* your Alex? Crown Prince...what-
ever?'

'Apparently.'

Her throat had dried like an arid desert. She
picked up the wine and gulped it down as if it were
a glass of water, grimacing as it hit her tastebuds.

Her brain was in overdrive. Tiny words, tiny
phrases, looks that had fleeted across his face and
disappeared in an instant. Tiny pieces of a jigsaw
puzzle she'd had no idea even existed.

A close-up picture of Alex emerging from a plane
appeared on the screen and she gasped. He looked
awful. He was still handsome, but his tanned skin

was pale and there were lines around his eyes—even their blueness had dimmed.

He hadn't called. He hadn't left a message at all. At first she'd been irritated. Then, she'd been angry. Finally, she'd admitted to herself she was devastated.

But this was something else entirely. Her fairytale in Paris had never included a real live prince.

Polly started chattering in her ear. 'No wonder you were miserable. What a catch. Ruby—you kissed a *prince*!' She stared back at the screen. 'I wonder what's going on.'

The newsreader interrupted the next report mid-story. 'We're going to cross live now to Euronia for an announcement.'

A sombre-faced grey-haired, black-suited man stood on a podium. A sign appeared beneath him: 'Palace Principale'.

'What does that mean?' asked Polly.

'I have no idea.' Ruby shook her head.

The man started speaking. 'After consultation with the Crown Council, the principality of Euronia would like to announce that, with immediate effect, Crown Prince Alexander de Castellane will be taking over as Regent of Euronia as His Majesty King Leopold is no longer able to exercise his royal functions. The Crown Prince Alexander will now be known as Prince Regent.'

The picture cut back to the newsreader as he glanced up from reading the piece of paper in his hands. 'There are unconfirmed reports that King Leopold has suffered a catastrophic stroke, but no one at the palace is willing to comment on his medical condition. We'll bring you an update whenever we get one.'

Polly turned to face Ruby. 'Wow. Just...*wow*.'

Ruby felt sick. Her heart had squeezed when she'd seen the expression on Alex's face. How on earth must he be feeling?

She wanted to be angry with him—she really did. Why couldn't he have told her who he really was?

But deep down she knew the answer to that.

A real live prince wouldn't be looking for a girl like her.

Not in this lifetime anyway.

# CHAPTER ONE

*Ten years later*

'RUBY?' THE DEPARTMENT receptionist shouted at her again.

Too many things were circulating in her brain. She needed to refer one child to someone else, another to an oral surgeon, and speak to the dietician about another.

She turned round and was nearly knocked over by a giant flower display. Her stomach tied itself up in little knots.

Rena smiled as she tried to hold up the giant display. 'You've got flowers again. Even more gorgeous than the last time. And, oh, *so* expensive.' She looked thoughtful for a moment. 'It's been a little while since the last bunch. Do you realise that, on and off, it's been six years you've been getting these mysterious flowers? Right from when you started here. Surely you must have guessed by now who they're from?'

Ruby shook her head. 'I have no idea. The cards never say anything specific.' She pulled out the latest one. 'See? *"Thinking of you and wishing you well."'*

Rena frowned at the card in her hands. 'Have

you tried phoning the florist to find out who sent them?' She was a regular amateur detective and could usually find a missing set of case notes in less than five minutes.

'Of course I have. But these places are used to things like this. They don't give anything away.'

'Well, whoever it is, money certainly isn't an object. These must have cost a fortune.' Rena reached up and touched one of the coloured petals. 'They smell gorgeous.' She frowned. 'Who have you seen lately that could have sent these?' She paused and bit her lip. 'Maybe it's Paul? Maybe he's trying for a reunion?'

Ruby shook her head. 'Paul would never send flowers like these.' Then she smiled. 'Paul would never send flowers full-stop. Which is why we're not together any more. That, and a whole lot of other things.'

Paul could never live up to the memory of Alex. Sometimes it felt like a figment of her imagination. Something so special that only she could remember. The only person she ever spoke to about it was Polly.

She'd tried to forget about him—she really had. She'd even lived with a lovely guy called Luke for a couple of years. But things just hadn't worked out between them, and in her heart she knew why. No matter how hard she tried, she just couldn't forget about her mysterious prince.

Rena smiled and touched Ruby's arm. 'Well,

you've obviously got a devoted, secret admirer. It's romantic. It's mysterious. I could probably work it into a book somewhere.'

Ruby laughed. 'Rena, you write about murder and mayhem. I'm not sure I want to end up in one of your books!'

She cast her eyes over the flowers again. Stunning. Really stunning. Beautiful tropical colours. Red, pinks, yellows and oranges. Like a burst of sunshine on a rainy day.

She swallowed. The flowers had stopped for a few years. Right around the time when it had been all over the news that Prince Alex had married Princess Sophia of Leruna. A perfect fairytale princess. Dainty and blonde—nothing like Ruby. A baby had followed quickly afterwards. Followed by her tragic death due to breast cancer.

All that crammed into the space of two years. And not a single bunch of flowers over that time.

The coincidence played on her mind. The deliveries had started again around eighteen months ago. Could the flowers have been from Alex all along?

Something coiled deep inside her.

She walked over to the window and stared outside at the pouring rain of London. Another wasted five minutes thinking about her prince.

*Her prince*. What a joke. She'd never used those words out loud and never would. It was bad enough that they circulated around her brain.

Alex might have had tragedy, but he'd also had a

life. Promotion for Ruby had come at a price. She'd been working so hard these last few years. Trying to change the lives of children who had been born with speech difficulties. It had left no time for her, no time for relationships, and no time to think about having a family.

The responsibilities of being in charge of a department in one of the best hospitals in London were relentless.

Sometimes she felt like a hamster, running in a wheel that she could never get off.

A porter brushed past, sending the scent of the beautiful flowers to meet her. It brought her back to reality quickly.

There was no point dreaming. She was nobody's princess.

And it was time to get back to work.

She was dashing around like a mad woman. Everyone in this hospital was the same. It had taken five different attempts for him to finally get some directions.

He stopped for a second to breathe. Ten years. Ten years since that night in Paris.

How different his life might have been. If his father hadn't been taken ill he would have met Ruby a few hours later in Paris and taken her sightseeing. That thought still made his stomach tighten.

She looked almost the same. Her dark curls were a little shorter. Her figure was just as curvy. But the expression on her face was more serious. Tired, even. And there were little lines around her eyes.

He didn't even want to look in the mirror lately. Although only ten years had passed since they'd last seen each other he was sure he'd aged about twenty.

The flowers he'd sent were sitting on the desk behind her. She wasn't even looking at them. Everyone else was oohing and aahing over them. But Ruby was too busy. Ruby was focused.

He watched her hurry around; she had a pile of cards in her hands.

'Seventeen new referrals,' she said to a nearby colleague, 'and Caroline is stuck in a traffic jam in the middle of London. How on earth are we going to get all these children assessed?'

He sucked in a breath. He'd never doubted for a second that Ruby would be dedicated to her work. But would it stand in the way of what he wanted her to do?

She tucked a curl behind her ear. It made his fingers tingle. *He'd* done that once.

'Can I help you?' someone asked him.

He shook his head. It was now or never.

He stepped forward. 'One of those referral cards will be from me.'

Ruby spun around to face him. The professional mask fell as quickly as the cards from her hand. His accent was unmistakable; she couldn't fail to recognise it.

'Alex,' she said. Nothing else. Her eyes locked on to his.

'Ruby.'

She tilted her head to the side, as if she were contemplating a million different questions, before sucking in a deep breath and giving a visible little shake of her head.

Ten years. Ten years since he'd run his fingers through those soft dark curls and looked into those chocolate-brown eyes. Ten years since he'd felt the silky softness of her skin, tasted the sweetness of her lips.

Every sensation, every touch, every taste flashed in front of him in an instant.

But Ruby wasn't caught in the same spell that he was.

She bent down to retrieve the cards and he knelt to help her. It was inevitable that their hands touched as they reached out towards the same card.

She pulled her hand away as if she'd been stung. 'Why, Alex? Why are you here?'

It was as if someone had reached into his chest and twisted his heart. There it was. In a few simple words a whole multitude of hurt. No one else would hear it. No one else would understand. But Ruby's deep brown eyes were fixed on his and he could see everything there. She looked wounded. Ten years on and her hurt was still easily visible.

But what did she see when she looked at him? He wasn't Alex the twenty-four-year-old any more—the bachelor Crown Prince with the world at his feet. He was a father. He was a widower. He was Prince Regent. The Prince continually in waiting.

And he was desperate.

In his head this had all been so easy. *Find someone you would trust with your daughter. Find Annabelle the expert help she needs.*

It had even seemed sensible to the palace advisors. If they'd questioned his choice of therapist at first, once they'd researched Ruby's qualifications and seen her recent publications all queries had vanished.

But now he was here in the flesh it was so much harder. Now he could see her. Now he could hear her. Now he could smell her. Her light floral scent was drifting around him.

He'd had no idea of the effect seeing Ruby again would have on him. Ten years… Ten years lost. Ten years of what might have been.

'Alex?'

The word jolted him and he smiled. No one called him Alex any more. No one had ever really called him just Alex.

He straightened up and handed her the final cards.

'I'm here because I need your help, Ruby.'

Any minute now a bunch of unicorns would come cantering along the hospital corridor, with exploding rainbows all around them.

She'd dreamt about Alex before. But never like this. Never in her workplace. All those dreams had been set back in Paris. Or in the Euronian palace that she'd looked at online.

But Alex standing in front of her at work, asking for her help…? She was obviously losing her mind.

He reached out and touched her bare arm. Short sleeves were essential in a hospital environment, to stop the spread of infection. This time she didn't pull away. This time she let the feel of the pads of his fingers spread warmth through her chilled arm.

He was really here.

This wasn't a strange hallucination due to overwork or lack of chocolate.

Ten years she'd waited to talk to this man again. Ten years waiting to ask him what the hell had happened back in Paris and why he'd never contacted her.

Alex—her Alex. *Her prince* was finally standing right in front of her.

He was every bit as handsome as she remembered. Better, even.

Tanned skin, dark hair and bright blue eyes. She'd sometimes wondered if she'd imagined how blue they were. But she hadn't. If anything she'd underestimated their effects. But, then again, she'd never seen Alex in daylight.

She wasn't imagining any of this. All six foot four of him was standing right in front of her.

Her eyes lowered to where his hand was touching

her. Tiny electric pulses were shooting up her arm. She didn't know whether to cry or be sick.

Every part of her imagination had just turned into reality.

In a way, it was a relief. She *had* met Alex. He *did* remember her. So why was that making her so darn angry right now?

He pulled his hand back from her arm and she lifted her head, pulling her shoulders back. *He'd taken his hand away.* And it had left her feeling bereft. Now she was feeling angry with herself. She didn't have a sensible thought in her head right now.

She swallowed and looked him in the eye. 'How can I help you, Alex?' The words were automatic. It was all she could manage right now.

He looked around. 'Is there somewhere we can talk?'

She nodded and gestured with her arm for him to walk down the corridor, stopped at a door, pulled a key from her pocket and unlocked the door.

Her office. It even had her name on the door: 'Ruby Wetherspoon, Head of Speech and Language'. She'd done well. Most days she was proud. Today she had no idea how she felt.

The office was small, but neat and tidy. She pointed to a chair and invited him to sit. It was almost a relief to sit at the other side of the desk and have the heavy wooden structure between them.

'How exactly do you think I can be of assistance to you, Alex?'

Her words were formal, her professional façade slipping back into place. The juggling of the cards on the table-top was the only sign of her nerves. She hoped he wouldn't notice.

'It's not me. It's my daughter Annabelle. She's three years old now and she isn't speaking.'

Ruby nodded automatically. His daughter. Of course. Why else would be come to her?

She had this sort of conversation every day. This one wouldn't be much different.

'Three years old is still an acceptable age for speech development. All children develop at a different rate. Some children have a delay in their speech and language development. Have you had her hearing checked?'

He sighed. She was going back to basics—which was the correct thing for a health professional. But she could tell from his expression he'd heard it all before.

'I've had ten different professional opinions on Annabelle. The latest of which is selective mutism. Her hearing is fine. Her comprehension is fine. She doesn't seem to *want* to speak.'

She could feel herself bristle. Ten assessments on a child? Talk about overkill. Why not just let her develop at her own pace? She tried to be pragmatic.

'How does she communicate with those around her?'

'She signs.'

Ruby was surprised. 'Proper signing?'

He nodded. 'We have a member of staff who's deaf. She's been able to sign since she was young.'

It wasn't particularly unusual in children who were deaf, or in children who had deaf siblings. But it *was* unusual in a child who could apparently hear and speak.

She lifted her hands. 'Then maybe she thinks that's normal?'

He shook his head.

It was time to ask some more questions.

'Has Annabelle ever spoken? Ever said a few words?'

'Only on a few select occasions.'

Strange… Ruby couldn't help but be a little curious. Selective mutism was certainly unusual but she'd dealt with a few cases before. She'd even published some professional papers on it.

Ruby lowered her voice. 'Does she speak to you, Alex?'

The question was straight to the heart of the matter. It was a natural question for any health professional, but she saw him recoil. She'd seen this before. He felt this was his fault. She'd dealt with lots of parents who felt guilty about whatever issue their child had. Most of the time it was just hard luck. Genetics. A developmental delay. A head injury or similar accident.

She asked the most practical question. 'Does Annabelle have anything significant in her medical history?'

'No. Nothing.'

They sat in silence for a few seconds. She couldn't take it. She couldn't take it a second longer. Her professional façade was slipping. After all this time—just to turn up like this and expect her to help him—just because he asked? Did she have *mug* stamped across her forehead?

She couldn't even acknowledge the flutters in her stomach. She couldn't even explain her feeling when she'd heard his voice and turned to see him again after all this time. It had been like a sucker punch.

It was time to stop being so polite.

Ruby leaned back in her chair. 'I don't get it, Alex. After all this time, why come to me? Why come here? You must have plenty of people in Euronia willing to help with your daughter.'

His brow was lined with deep furrows that marred his handsome face. It made her feel self-conscious. She only had the lightest dusting of make-up on, to emphasise her brown eyes and pink lips. How much had she changed in the last ten years? Would he be disappointed by what he saw?

Why was he here? Why, after all this time, had he been convinced that this was the right thing to do?

'I want to feel as if I've tried everything possible for Annabelle. I haven't had faith in any of the people who have seen her and assessed her. And, whilst the latest diagnosis seems reasonable, I'm not happy at the treatment plan for Annabelle.'

*Maybe that's because you should have left her*

*alone to be a normal toddler.* Ruby was still imagining what ten assessments had done to that poor child. But she couldn't say those words out loud.

It was difficult. This was Alex, her mysterious Frenchman—who wasn't a Frenchman after all. She'd never thought she'd come into contact with him for *work*. She never thought she'd come into contact with him again.

'What *is* the treatment plan for Annabelle?'

He pushed a folder he'd been carrying across the desk towards her. She opened it and scanned it quickly. Whilst the assessment might have been thorough, she didn't agree at all with what was in the plan, or with the conclusions it had already surmised.

Ever the professional, she raised her head and selected her words carefully. 'Every professional will have a different idea of the correct plan for your daughter. It's not really my place to disagree.'

He pointed to the file. 'What would *you* do?'

She opened her mouth automatically to speak, then closed it again. 'What does it matter?'

'Because I'd like you to come to Euronia and assess Annabelle for yourself. I'd like you to be the one to plan her care and treat her.'

He might as well have dumped a bucket of ice-cold water over her head. She was stunned. 'That's impossible.'

'No. It's not. I know you have a job here, and patients, but I've offered your Director of Services a generous annual bequest if you'll agree to come and work for me—for Annabelle,' he added quickly.

'What?' She stood up, the chair behind her flying backwards. 'You've done *what*?'

She couldn't believe her ears. The tiny glimmer of hope that he'd searched her out for any reason other than his daughter died in an instant. He might be a prince in another country, but he didn't seem much like a prince to her now.

'And you did that without speaking to me first?' She walked around the desk, reached down, and grabbed hold of his jacket, pulling him to his feet. 'How dare you, Alex? How *dare* you? Ten years later you think you can just walk into my life and *buy* me?'

Anger and the untold resentment that had festered for ten years came spilling out. This wasn't her. She never acted like this. But she just couldn't help it.

She shook her head fiercely, blazing with fury. 'You can't buy me, Alex. I'm not for sale.' She held out one hand. 'I have a job. Responsibilities. I have staff to take care of—patients to take care of.'

She stared at her other hand, still gripping tightly to the lapel of his jacket. What on earth was she doing? Her knuckles were white and she quickly loosened her grip and took a step backwards. Her heart was thudding in her chest. Her head was thumping.

'And you could do it better if you had two more

permanent members of staff.' He cut her off before she had more time to think about it.

Her mouth fell open. 'What?'

'That's what I promised your director. Permanent funding for two more members of staff if they'll release you to work with Annabelle. Plus filling your post while you're gone.'

Her brain was whizzing. Two more members of staff could make a world of difference to this place. Time. It would give her staff time. The one thing she couldn't conjure up for them.

She hated rushing assessments. She hated not having enough time to allocate to the children who needed her. She hated having to turn children away because there just wasn't enough space for any more patients. Two more members of staff was a luxury she couldn't afford to ignore.

'Why on earth would you do this?'

He sat back down in his seat and put his head in his hands.

She'd read about everything that had happened to him in the last ten years. Now here he was, right in front of her, and she actually felt sorry for him.

She started shaking her head. 'It feels like blackmail, Alex. I haven't seen you in ten years. *Ten years!* Not a word from you—nothing. And now this.' She started pacing around the small office. 'I know what happened to your father. The whole world knows. But you never contacted me. You never said anything. I was left sitting in that hotel for two days, wondering if I'd imagined everything. Thank goodness Polly dragged me out and about.'

His head shot up. 'I did contact you. I sent a message.'

'I never got any message!' She was still angry.

'But I sent one. My head of security—he took it to the hotel. Gave it to the reception clerk. You *must* have got it.'

She shook her head and lowered her voice. 'There was no message, Alex. None. I waited and waited.'

She hated the way the words made her feel. She hated the way she wanted to reach out and grab them. Grab the fact that Alex *had* tried to reach her—no matter what else had happened in his life. But it was the expression on his face that was worse. He looked hurt. He looked injured.

But, most importantly, he looked tired.

She knelt down in front of him. His father had been sick for ten years. He had a country to run. His wife had died from cancer—she was assuming he'd nursed her through that—and he had a daughter whom he clearly loved but needed help with.

She reached up and touched his hand. Her skin coming into contact with his almost made her smile. Her pale skin against his tanned skin. A world of difference.

The sensation she felt touching his skin was still there. Still electrifying. But she had to put a reality check on things.

She spoke quietly. 'Why now, Alex? Why me?'

It was only a few words but they meant so much more than she was actually saying. He knew that. He must.

He reached up and touched her cheek. *Zing*.

'Because there is no one else. No one else I could trust with the thing that is most precious to me.'

She blinked, trying to stop the tears forming in her eyes.

Nothing about wanting to see her again. Nothing about wanting to know how she was.

But he had just told her he trusted her with the thing most precious in the world to him. His daughter.

She didn't know whether to be happy or sad.

He pulled a picture from his wallet. A sad-looking blonde-haired toddler. She was beautiful. Just like her mother had been. But she wasn't laughing. She wasn't playing. She didn't look happy.

'Oh, Alex...' she breathed.

'Will you come?' His voice sounded as if it was breaking.

She stood up, her mind whirling. 'I'll need to think about it. You'll need to give me some time.'

How ironic. Ten years later she was asking him for time.

How on earth could she not do this? The picture of the little girl had broken her heart. She had no idea if she could help or not—but she could try.

Outside her office she could see figures rushing past. The hospital was always busy—never enough time to do everything. It was wearing her down. She loved her job, but the truth was she'd spent the last few months searching the vacancy bulletins.

One thing. If she did this one thing she could help this department and these kids for ever. Was it really such a hard task?

A chair scraped along the floor behind her. Alex had stood up, a resigned look on his face. He nodded at the desk, 'I'll leave those things for you to look at. My contact details are there. Let me know when you make up your mind.'

He thought she was going to say no. And right now that was the way she was leaning. What would she do with her flat—her cat—if she left to go abroad?

The file and the photo of Annabelle sat on her desk. He had his hand on the door handle.

'Alex? How did you know where I was?'

It had bothered her since he'd first arrived.

His bright blue eyes fixed on hers. It was the first time she'd seen anything resembling the eyes she'd looked into ten years ago.

'I've always known where you were, Ruby,' he said quietly as he opened the door and walked down the corridor.

# CHAPTER TWO

THE PLANE JOURNEY was smooth. The private jet immaculate. Any other person might have taken the opportunity to relax, but Ruby's stomach had been jittery ever since they'd left London.

She stared out of the window as the plane came into land. Her first sight of Euronia. A stunning, winding coastline overlooking the Mediterranean Sea. A population of two hundred thousand people over an area of only seventy kilometres. The rich and famous flocked here because of the tax benefits. The press loved Euronia because it seemed to host every celebrity wedding that had ever existed.

The plane landed quickly and glided to a halt on the Tarmac. She hadn't spoken to Alex since she'd seen him at the hospital. The number he'd given her had been for his secretary—a chirpy little man who'd been delighted when she'd said she would come to Euronia and had spoken with great fondness about Annabelle. He'd arranged everything. Even advising on what kind of clothing to bring and asking her for her dress and shoe size so he could provide some extra items if required.

The pilot and the stewardess had both been polite but formal. She wondered if they were used to fading into the background.

A black limousine was waiting for her.

'Welcome to Euronia, Ms Wetherspoon. It will only take ten minutes to reach the palace. Please make yourself comfortable and help yourself to refreshments.'

Another man in black. She hid her smile. Any minute now she would hear the theme tune to that movie in her head. It was the same garb that the men in Paris had been wearing all those years ago. Those men had made her uncomfortable. This man was a little different. His eyes were scanning the horizon constantly. Was he a chauffeur or security?

She settled into the comfortable leather seats. The 'refreshments' in front of her were wine, champagne and beer. It was ten-thirty in the morning. What she'd actually like was a cup of tea.

She watched the scenery speed past.

Polly's words echoed in her ears. *This isn't a movie. He's using you, Ruby. Don't get any ideas about this at all.'*

Her disdain had been apparent as soon as she'd heard what had happened. Polly had long since abandoned any romantic notions of her prince. She'd been the one to see exactly how devastated Ruby had been. But it was all right for Polly. She'd got her happy-ever-after—a doting husband and a baby in her arms.

'How long will you be gone?' she'd asked Ruby moodily.

'I have no idea.' And she really didn't. She

couldn't plan anything until she'd assessed Anna-belle.

The car swept through some regal gates, past armed guards and down a long pale yellow sweeping drive. The view over the Mediterranean was breathtaking.

No turning back. She was here now. She tugged at her pale green dress. It was a little more formal than what she normally wore, but at least it didn't crumple.

The palace came into view. Nicknamed the Pink Palace, the Palace Principale was built from pink and red sandstone. She'd seen pictures on the internet, but seeing it in reality was entirely different.

Ruby took a deep breath. There must be a million little girls' birthday cakes all over the world based on this palace. Four square turrets and it seemed like hundreds of slim windows looked down on her. The palace doors were enormous, with wide sweeping steps leading up to them.

Intimidating. Definitely intimidating.

She would be lying if she claimed she'd never thought about this. Of course she had. Every girl had.

But every girl hadn't kissed a prince.

*Oh, boy.* She squeezed her eyes shut for a second. This was harder than she'd thought.

Actually being here in Euronia was much harder than she'd imagined it to be.

In her head this was a job. This was professional.

So why was her heart fluttering so much? And why did she want to run back along that yellow driveway?

A man was standing at the top of the steps to greet her. It wasn't Alex. Of course it wasn't Alex. He hadn't even spoken to her on the phone.

She climbed the steps and looked out over the Mediterranean Sea. Lots of little white boats bobbed up and down on the beautiful blue water. *Little* boats? They probably cost more than she would earn in her lifetime. This was a whole other world.

But she was here to do a job, not to admire the scenery—no matter how beautiful it was.

The sooner she got started the better.

He watched her step from the car. She was picture-perfect. Her elegant legs were the first hint of what was to come as her slim figure emerged in a pale green dress that fluttered around her in the strong sea winds. It was an occupational hazard of having a palace on the sea.

His mother had always joked that one day a press photographer would get a picture of something they shouldn't. She'd been born before her time, and had been taken much too soon. She would have known exactly what to do with Annabelle.

He watched as Rufus, his private secretary, bustled around about Ruby. He would probably give her a headache in the first five minutes, but his heart was in the right place.

Rufus had organised everything once he'd known Ruby would be coming. From her favourite foods and TV shows to her clothes—everything would be taken care of. The only thing he'd asked for some input with was where to put her in the palace.

Alex hadn't been quite sure, but had finally decided she should be in the West Wing, overlooking the sea. The rooms there had always been his mother's favourites.

It only took a few moments before his phone rang.

'Your Majesty? I'm afraid there's a problem with our guest. Her accommodation is unsuitable. She's requesting rooms next to Princess Annabelle.' Rufus was so overwrought he was practically squeaking.

'Take her to the library. I'll be along directly.'

Five minutes. That was all it had taken for Ruby to cause turmoil in his life. He just hoped this wasn't a decision he'd live to regret.

He strode down the stairs and along the corridor towards the library. Rufus was flapping around the doorway. He wasn't used to people not going along with his plans.

'Where is she?' Alex looked around the empty room.

'She went upstairs to Princess Annabelle's quarters. She knows Annabelle isn't there but she said she wanted to make herself familiar with the place.'

Rufus cringed. The whole thing was probably giving him palpitations. It didn't take much these days.

Alex waved his hand. 'Leave this to me.'

He didn't need Rufus getting over-excited. What on earth was Ruby *doing*? She'd barely put her feet across the front door.

He bit his lip as he climbed the stairs at a rapid pace. She wasn't used to things like this. Maybe he should try and exercise a little patience. Ruby wasn't used to royal palaces and protocols. She was here because he'd asked her to be. She might have a job to do, but she was also his guest.

He reached Annabelle's rooms quickly. The door was open wide, giving a clear view of the palace gardens and the sea. Ruby was sitting on one of the window seats, but she wasn't admiring the view. One of Annabelle's stuffed toys was in her hands. It was a koala left by the Australian ambassador after his last visit. Ruby was looking around the room carefully.

He stood behind her, looking at her outline, seeing every curve of her body. It sent a rush of blood around his own body.

He hadn't quite imagined how this would feel. Ruby, sitting in his palace, with the backdrop he'd looked at every day for years behind her. It almost seemed unreal.

'Ruby, what are you doing in here?'

She sighed and turned to face him. The first thing that struck him was her big brown eyes. So dark, so deep, so inviting... He really needed to get hold of himself.

'There are rooms right next door to Annabelle's. It would be best if I stayed there.'

'Why?' The rooms he'd chosen for her in the West Wing were brighter, more spacious. The ones next to Annabelle were smaller, usually reserved for staff. 'The other rooms are nicer. They have more space.'

She waved her hand. She didn't look happy. Was she already regretting coming here?

'I need to be next to her, Alex. You forget—I live in London. These rooms will be a penthouse compared to my flat. I need to see her, Alex. I need to see her in her own environment. I need to see how she functions. I need to see how she communicates with those around her. She's three. I need to watch her in the place where she's most comfortable. I'm not just here to assess whether she can actually speak or not. I need to assess her ability to understand—her cognitive abilities. I need to see how she interacts with those around her.'

She held out her arm across the immaculately kept room.

'Is this Annabelle's world?'

There was tinge of sadness to her words. As if to her the beautiful rooms were clearly lacking.

'Where is she now?'

Professional Ruby. The one he'd never really experienced before. She wasn't having wishful thoughts about *him*. She was concentrating on the job she was here to do.

He glanced at his watch. 'She's with her nanny. She goes to the local nursery for a few hours twice a week. Her nanny thought mixing with other children might be good for her. She's due back any minute.'

Ruby nodded and smiled.

Alex continued. 'This isn't a big country. Annabelle will go to the local school with the other children, just like I did. My father always believed that to lead the people you had to be part of the people.'

'He sounds like a very wise man.' She turned and looked out over the sea. 'Where is your father? Is he here?'

He hesitated. They kept details about King Leopold closely guarded. But this was Ruby. He trusted her with the details of his daughter—why not his father?

'He's not here. He's in Switzerland.'

'Switzerland?'

'His stroke was severe. We have a hospital in Euronia, but we don't have ICU facilities.'

She walked towards him, concern lacing her brow. Clearly no one had told her about the protocol of remaining ten steps away from the Prince. He was glad. He could see a tiny smattering of freckles across the bridge of her nose. Had they been there before?

If asked, he would have said that every part of her face had been etched on his brain. But these were new. It was disconcerting. A part of Ruby he hadn't kept in his head.

She put her hand on his chest. He could practically hear the alarms going off around the building.

'Ten years on your father still needs ICU facilities?'

He was trying not to concentrate on her warm skin penetrating through his shirt. 'Yes—and no. He did at first. His recovery was limited and slow. He was moved to a specialist rehab unit. But now he has frequent bouts of pneumonia and he needs assistance with breathing. He has to be kept near an ICU. Euronia doesn't have those facilities.'

'You could get them.'

Her voice was quiet. She knew exactly what she was saying. It was enough. The rest of the words didn't have to be said out loud. No one else around him would do this.

'I could,' he said gently. 'But my father wouldn't want people to see him the way he is now. It would break his heart.' His voice was strained. Even he could hear it.

It was so strange to have Ruby standing right here in front of him, in his daughter's room. He'd imagined her in many different scenarios over the years, but this had never been one of them.

In his darkest moments, when everything had seemed insurmountable, he'd always been able to close his eyes and go back to Paris, the fireworks and Ruby.

A perfect night. With a disastrous end.

She'd suited her red coat and hat that cold night. And for the last ten years that was the way he'd remembered her.

Ruby—with the sparkle in her eyes, the flirtatious laugh and the easy chatter. Every time he thought of her there were fireworks in the background. Fireworks that matched her personality and her vitality.

But today, in the sun, the pale green chiffon complemented her dark brown curls and brown eyes. The dress covered every part of her it should, but he hadn't expected her to look quite so elegant.

It was just the two of them. No palace staff. No interruptions.

'I've met so many different people, Ruby. I see masks, façades, the whole time. I've never seen any of that with you. Ten years ago I saw someone who was devastated at not getting her dream job—someone who wasn't afraid to say that to a stranger. All the people who have assessed Annabelle…'

He shook his head.

'None of them have felt genuine to me. Oh, they might be professionals in their field. They might have letters after their names. But most of them only tell me what they think I want to hear. Others try and blind me with science. I don't think any of them have ever wanted to find out who the real Annabelle is. They might be interested in the theory or psychology of why a three-year-old won't talk…'

He put his hand on his chest, directly over hers. One set of fingers intertwined with another.

'But none of them have cared in *here* about why she isn't speaking.'

He could lean forward right now. He could lean forward and capture her lips the way he did ten years ago.

Ruby's eyes were fixed on his. 'Well, no wonder.'

'No wonder what?'

'No wonder you came looking for me.'

# CHAPTER THREE

IT TOOK ANNABELLE four long days to acknowledge Ruby's existence. At first she completely ignored her, preferring to communicate in her own way with her nanny.

The nanny, Brigette, was thankfully a dedicated and sensible woman. She'd spent all her life in Euronia and had been with the family since Annabelle's arrival. The little girl trusted her completely, but once Brigette realised Ruby was here to stay and help with Annabelle it was clear she was glad of the assistance. She loved the little girl but felt frustrated that she wasn't able to help more.

Ruby was patient. But Alex was hovering around her constantly, asking her questions, destroying her concentration and patience. Any time he appeared her senses went into overdrive. The timbre of his voice, the accent, could make her legs turn to mush.

She had to drive a little bit of her anger back into her head. Her anger that she was here for Annabelle—not for Alex. It didn't matter that it might be irrational. It was the only thing currently keeping her sane.

He appeared at her shoulder, his scent drifting around her. She didn't even turn around.

'Alex, you need to leave me to get on with the job. That's what I'm here to do.'

Annabelle was playing quietly in her room. Flitting between colouring at the table and drawing chalk pictures on her board. There was a television in her room, which she rarely watched, and a tablet on the chair next to her.

She was definitely an interesting study. She was a creative little girl. The drawers at her desk were filled with cardboard, paint, ribbon, glitter and glue. She was never happier than when she was covered in the stuff. But the life of a royal princess meant that she was continually being cleaned, tidied and paraded elsewhere.

The only time she showed interest in the tablet—which she could use easily—was when she watched clips of singing and dancing from films. *Annie*, *The Sound of Music* and *Seven Brides for Seven Brothers* seemed to be the favourites.

There was a mixture of melancholy and frustration that emanated from Alex when he watched Annabelle.

'But I'm her *parent*. Aren't you supposed to talk to me and give me a report?'

Ruby nodded and gave a little sigh. 'I suppose… But I haven't finished my full assessment of Annabelle yet. I can only give you my first impressions.'

She turned around to face him, conscious of the fact that she'd be subjected to his killer blue eyes.

'This will take longer than I thought. I have to

wait until Annabelle is ready to communicate with me—to work with me. I'm not going to force myself on her. She's not that type of kid.'

The smile that spread across his face was one of complete relief. He put his warm hands on her shoulders. '*That's* why you're here, Ruby. You're the first person who's assessed Annabelle that has said that to me. You don't care about the time span. You care about the child.'

*Because you're paying me to.*

It was an uncomfortable thought racing around in her brain. She was used to working for the health service. She'd never seen private patients before. Every child she'd assessed had been given the best possible assessment. But the health services were pushed for time and it sometimes frustrated her. Here she didn't have those worries.

Everything about this was a whole new experience. Staying in a palace. Knowing that after ten years she might bump into Alex at any second. The *you're paying me to* thought had a tiny bit of self-preservation about it. It kept things in perspective. It kept her grounded. It reminded her why she was actually here.

Alex was still touching her shoulders. She was wearing a sundress and his fingers were in direct contact with her skin. The sensations that were currently running like little pulses down her arms were conflicting with all her previous thoughts.

'Why don't we do this somewhere else?

'What?'

*Do what somewhere else?* She felt panic rush through her. How exactly had she been looking at him?

He lifted his hand from her shoulder and waved it towards the window. 'I've not been a very good host. Let me show you a little of Euronia.' He looked down at her sandals. 'How do you feel about a walk?'

Her sandals were pretty, but flat and comfortable. Her curiosity had definitely flared. 'I feel fine about a walk.'

'Then let's go.'

'Don't you need to let your security team know first, Alex?'

He smiled again and shook his head. 'You know, you're the only person that actually calls me that.'

'What?'

'Alex. No one else calls me that.'

She shook her head in disbelief. 'What on earth *do* they call you?'

He shrugged. 'Prince Regent or Your Majesty. If it's someone I've known a long time they might call me Alexander.'

A different world.

She stepped right up to him, her nose only inches away from his. 'But I know you as Alex. Always have. Always will.'

He smiled and gestured for her to follow him,

and led her down a huge array of corridors and out through one of the back doors of the castle.

The gardens were beautiful—colourful and perfectly groomed. She recognised the marble fountain from an old black and white picture she had seen of Alex and his future wife as children.

They walked across the immaculate expanse of green lawn towards the city. It was officially the smallest city in the world—not much bigger than an average town. But it had grown exponentially as the economy of Euronia had grown.

'Did you play in these gardens when you were a child?'

He nodded. 'Yes. There's a secret maze in the forest over there. And my father ordered a tree house to be built and it took the carpenter nearly a whole year.' He gave a little sigh. 'Annabelle is still a little young to play in it. I don't even think she'll like it.'

'Haven't you ever shown it to her?'

He shook his head. 'I've been too focused on other things when it comes to Annabelle. We haven't got around to anything like that.'

Ruby nodded and bit her tongue. It was important that she find out about the relationship between Alex and his daughter. It wouldn't do well for her to criticise, but she could already imagine the kind of recommendations she might make.

'Well, if you show it to me some time maybe I can give you some suggestions on how to make it more appealing to a little girl.'

He gave a little nod as they approached a gate in the high walls. Alex keyed in a code and the door swung open.

'Won't that set off alarms everywhere?'

'No. It's my code. They'll know it's me that's opened the door.'

The back entrance opened directly on to the sea cliffs. The breeze was startlingly stiff and she shivered. She should have brought a cardigan, but the light summer breezes on the castle balcony had been pleasing.

Her bright pink dress whipped around in the wind and Alex pulled off his jacket and put it over her shoulders. The first thing she noticed was the smell of his aftershave as she slid her arms into the jacket and pulled it around her.

'Do you do this often?'

'Of course.' He raised his eyebrows. 'Do you think I spend all my time holed up in the castle?'

'I have no idea, Alex. I have no idea what you do at all.'

She heard him suck in a breath. She wasn't trying to bring up the past, but if she wanted to help Annabelle she had to have a good idea about the environment in which she lived.

The walk into the centre of the city was pleasant. It was less than a mile and they browsed at the shop windows, with several of the shopkeepers coming out to speak to them. One gave Alex some cheese, another some ham wrapped in paper.

'Your favourite,' he said with a smile.

The clothing and jewellery shops were spectacular. No prices in any window. Ruby could only imagine how much things actually cost around here.

She was surprised at how relaxed everything was. The palace was much more formal. People nodded to Alex in the street, but no one seemed in awe of him.

They'd reached the casino in the middle of the city. 'Would you like to sample some of the best cake in Euronia?' he asked.

'Is it better than the cake in Paris?'

Their eyes met. It was a moment. A second for them both to remember that night ten years ago in Paris. Both of them were smiling, as if it were an automatic reaction to the memory.

He leaned forward a little, the heat from his body emanating towards her. 'The cake in Paris won't even come close to the cake in Euronia.'

She lifted her head. They were so close. 'Is that a promise?'

He slid his hand around her back and pulled out a chair for her. 'Absolutely.'

The café Alex had chosen was opposite the casino. She'd seen pictures of the place on the internet. Just about every visitor who came to Euronia visited this café and watched the coming and goings at the casino.

'Aren't you worried you'll get harassed here?'

He shook his head. 'It's Sunday. No cruise ships

moor at Euronia on a Sunday and no bus tours run. Today's the best day for me to take a walk around.'

The owner of the café appeared and nodded at Alex. 'The usual coffee and cake, Your Highness?' Alex nodded. 'And for the beautiful lady?'

'You should go and look in the glass cabinet. The cakes are amazing.'

Ruby stood up and walked over to the cabinet, spending a few minutes talking to the café owner before finally settling on a strawberry and cream sponge.

It was surreal. Sitting in the warm sunshine of Euronia with Alex.

These were the kind of things that had drifted into her imagination in the early days. Fanciful thoughts of what might have been.

Alex seemed happy here—more relaxed than he was in the palace, which was strange, as that was his home.

He drank his steaming coffee and devoured a piece of chocolate cake as soon as it appeared. He held out his fork towards her. 'Try some.'

She hesitated, then leaned forward, opening her mouth. 'Mmm, it's delicious. You're right. The cakes here *are* nicer than in Paris.'

He licked some chocolate from his lips and nodded towards her strawberry and cream sponge. 'What? All of them?'

She raised her eyebrows at him and waved her

fork. 'I'm warning you—Prince or no Prince. Touch my cake and I'll spear you with my fork.'

He threw back his head and laughed. 'I'm sure you offered me a piece of your cake in Paris.'

She winked at him as she took another bite. 'I might have. But I was trying to impress you then.' She smiled and shrugged. 'Those days are gone.'

'You're not trying to impress me now?'

'No,' she said solemnly. She reached one hand over to his. Her other one was poised carefully. 'I'm just trying to distract you so I can steal some more of your chocolate cake.'

Her fork swooped in and she grabbed another piece.

He held the hand resting over his. 'That's what I like about you, Ruby. What I remember. A girl who likes to eat cake.'

She licked her fork. 'It's my best talent. It's taken years and years of practice.'

She liked this. He was relaxed here. He was much more like the Alex she remembered. Around the palace he seemed so much more uptight.

'How long has the casino been open?' She watched the stream of people entering and leaving.

'Almost three hours.'

She glanced at her watch. 'But it's only one o'clock in the day. I thought gambling would be a night-time kind of thing.'

'Have you ever been to Las Vegas or Atlantic City?'

She shook her head. 'So people gamble here all day?'

He nodded.

'And is that good or bad?'

He fixed his blue eyes on hers. 'You mean for the people, or for the place?'

She shrugged, 'Both, I guess. I don't really know that much about gambling.'

'Neither do I. But tourism is one of the ways to bring money into Euronia. The new port means that cruise ships can easily moor here. We open up part of the castle for tours at different times of the year. We've spent money building five-star hotels that keep the rich and famous happy. And we have some of the most beautiful venues for weddings in the world. That, and the tax benefits, mean that Euronia thrives.'

She listened to his words carefully, hearing the underlying pride as he said them. Ten years ago there had been financial predictions that Euronia would have to be taken over by another country to remain viable. None of those predictions had come true.

'Is that why you went to Harvard and studied business—to find a way to help Euronia?'

He gave a rueful smile. 'If I'd had my way I would have gone to Harvard to study chemistry or physics.'

She sat back in her chair. 'Really? You like that kind of thing?'

He nodded. 'Of course I do. Doesn't every little

boy want to be an astronaut? I still want to. Science, maths or engineering—that's what you need a degree in.'

She couldn't help but smile. This was the Alex she'd met back in Paris. This was the guy who'd kissed her until her toes tingled. This was the guy she'd lost a tiny little piece of her heart to.

'You really looked into this?'

'Of course I did.'

She finished the last piece of her cake and licked the fork. It had been delicious. Now she knew this place existed she would try to take a daily trip.

He glanced towards her and it sent a tingle right down to her toes. A cheeky look, a flirtatious look, a maybe-none-of-those-things look, but there was no denying its effect.

It made her feel exposed. It made her feel as if all those fleeting thoughts, all those ridiculous daydreams about being here in Euronia, were being instantly read in her mind.

'Now I'm sold on the cake here I want to come back.'

'I'll bring you any time you like.'

'Good. Because I want you to bring us tomorrow.'

'Us?'

'Yes. You, me and Annabelle. I've watched her in the palace. Later on I'm going to watch her at nursery. But I also need to see how the two of you interact together.'

'But you've seen her with me in the last few days.'

'That was in the palace. This is different.' She held out her hands. 'This is normal.'

He raised his eyebrows at her. 'My life isn't normal?'

She sighed. 'No, Alex. Your life isn't normal. But Annabelle's should be. She's just a little girl. I want to see her come and eat cake or ice cream with her dad.'

If it was possible his tanned face paled. He took a few moments, and she could almost see the thoughts flickering across his face.

Alex had been so relaxed around her for the last hour. She was just praying that the palace portcullis wasn't about to come down, slamming into place.

He gave a slow nod and lifted his bright blue eyes to meet hers. He didn't get it. When he looked at her like that it was magnetising. She couldn't pull herself away if she tried.

She hated it that after ten years he could still do that to her. Still make her feel as if she was the only person around. Make all the noise and people around them just fade into the background.

Her mouth was instantly dry. She wanted to lick her lips, but was afraid of what that might suggest. It might let him know exactly what she was thinking. And none of her current thoughts could ever be acknowledged between them.

There was one way to break this spell.

'Tell me about your wife, Alex. Tell me about Annabelle's mother.'

*There.* He looked as if she'd just sucker-punched him. Truth be told, she really didn't want to talk to Alex about his wife. She didn't need to hear how beautiful or wonderful she'd been—the press had already let the world know that. She especially didn't want her stomach to clench so hard she might be sick.

But this was it. This was the way to stop her thinking about her prince. *Her prince.* She was still doing it. It was natural.

And this was a natural question to ask Alex. If she wanted to assess Annabelle properly she had to know the family circumstances.

'What do you want to know?' His voice was hoarse.

She signalled to the waiter. 'Can we have some water, please?' She needed to do something with her own scratchy throat.

The sun was shining down on them, warming her arms and legs. This should be perfect. She was sitting in the most gorgeous setting. From this café she could look across the square at the port and see million-dollar boats bobbing on the sea in front of her. Across from her was the guy she'd thought about for the last ten years.

But she'd just managed to ruin the mood completely. It was time to stop things being personal—it was time to be professional.

'What happened with Sophia? I've seen pictures of the two of you sitting on the fountain at the castle as children. You obviously knew her for a long time?'

He ran his fingers through his dark hair. She was conscious of the furrows in his brow, the lines around his eyes.

He took a deep breath. 'Sophia was my oldest friend. Even though she lived in a neighbouring country our fathers were constantly doing state business together. She was always here.'

Ruby sipped the water the waiter had brought. Nothing would get rid of the dryness in her throat. 'And…?'

He looked at her, then quickly looked away again—almost as if he was embarrassed to speak about Sophia in front of her.

She licked her lips. She wanted to tell him that she only needed to know about Annabelle. But her insides were churning. This was the moment when she'd hear the things she'd always known.

His voice had the slightest tremor. It was only because she was listening so intently that she noticed.

'Sophia came to me after everything had happened. After my father had had the stroke and I'd been made Prince Regent.' His hands went back to his hair. 'Things were a mess. I was totally consumed by finances, by looking for new opportunities for Euronia. But Sophia was sick. I knew it as soon as saw her.'

He sat back in his chair. His body was rigid. One hand clenched in a fist.

'I was furious. She hadn't told me anything.' He fixed his eyes on a point over her shoulder. 'The speculation was right. She had breast cancer. It was terminal. Sophia came and told me after she'd tried a number of treatments. She'd already made her mind up that she didn't want to do that any more.'

There was a sheen across his eyes and it made Ruby's heart ache for him. But down in the pit of her stomach there was something else. A tiny smattering of jealousy that he'd felt so much for this woman.

'So you got married?'

She tried to make it sound casual. But her voice was tight and she knew it. She just hoped he wouldn't notice.

Alex gave the slightest nod of his head.

'Sophia came to me. She told me her diagnosis. She told me the one thing she wanted in the world was to have a baby before it was too late. I couldn't say no to her. I just couldn't. I loved her. People had speculated for years that we would marry—but it never entered our heads. Sophia had plans—she had big plans. She was so creative…she loved art and design. But she also had a really inquisitive nature. She was torn between design and journalism. She loved to write. She had sketches and sketches of dress designs.'

He sighed,

'And then…' he lifted his hand '…the cancer.' He shook his head. 'It was as if all her dreams just evaporated. She'd already made up her mind before she came to see me. If we had a child together it would seal the fate of our two kingdoms. Sophia was an only child. When she died her whole dynasty would die with her. She didn't want that to happen.' His voice steadied. 'Neither of us wanted that to happen.'

He pressed his lips together.

'You probably already know this, but when Sophia's father dies Annabelle will be Queen of Leruna. If he dies before Annabelle comes of age I'll be Regent to the two principalities.'

His lifted his eyes and met her gaze full-on. The implications were huge. He was telling her he'd made a pact with his childhood friend. They'd married. They'd had a child together. They'd cemented their relationship and safeguarded the future of two countries. How noble.

She was trying hard not to be bitter. And there was still a tiny flicker of hope. He hadn't said Sophia was the love of his life. He'd said he loved her. That was different.

Ruby felt her voice wobble. 'She was really young to have breast cancer, Alex.'

'I know.' He paused. 'She had the gene.' It came out in a whisper.

Her breath caught in her throat. 'Sophia had the gene?' Everyone had heard about 'the gene' by now—the mutation linked with breast and ovarian cancer. 'What about Annabelle?'

He shook his head. 'I had her tested. She's not affected.'

Her breath left her in a whoosh. 'Oh, wow. You must be so relieved.' She toyed with the glass of water in her hands. 'I know it's a silly question, but was there nothing else they could do? It's just that... wouldn't the pregnancy have made a difference to her cancer? I thought they recommend that you don't get pregnant if you have that type of cancer?'

His face was serious. 'Sophia was very single-minded. She knew that she would die eventually. Having a child was the most important thing to her in the world. She could have had some type of chemotherapy while she was pregnant—but she refused. She did have some immediately following delivery. But she was so weak. So tired. She only took the treatment to prolong her time with Annabelle. Once she realised how sick it was making her, and how it really didn't make any difference to the outcome, she decided to stop everything. She wanted some time with Annabelle.'

'And did she have time with Annabelle?'

Ruby was trying to work out the impact on the child. Annabelle couldn't have been much more than a baby. Was there any chance that what had happened then might have had an impact on her future? It seemed unlikely. There was lots of debate as to when a child formed its first memories. Most researchers thought it happened around the age of three. But Ruby had seen a lot of things in her work that had made her question that.

'She had a few months. She spent every possible second with Annabelle. By the end she was just too tired, too sick. Annabelle was in her arms when she died. She was only eleven months old.'

'It must have been devastating for you.'

'She was my childhood friend—the person I grew up with. If my father hadn't had the stroke, if Sophia hadn't had breast cancer, lots of things might have been different.'

Something flickered across his eyes. A tiny moment of recognition. An awareness. A regret.

'I'm sorry, Ruby,' he whispered.

Tears filled her eyes. It was an acknowledgement, however brief, of what had happened between them. He was laying everything out on the table for her. It was just the two of them. No one else to interrupt. No one else to interfere.

He reached over and touched her cheek—just as he had all those years ago in Paris. He tucked a piece of hair behind her ear.

Silence. For the longest time. Lots of words unspoken.

His fingers stroked across her cheek. So many things wanted to spill out of her. But her frustration was dissipating. The years had passed. She couldn't be angry with him any more. She'd lived a whole ten years of her life without him. He'd always been in the background of her mind. No matter how hard she'd tried to push him away. But her memories of Alex were memories of one New Year's Eve and a moment in time.

The Alex she saw in front of her now was the one that really existed. A father. A prince with the responsibilities of a country—two countries. Someone who'd set aside his career ambitions to fulfil his duty to his country. Someone who'd just told her that he was sorry. That meant more than anything.

She'd been harbouring an illusion for the last ten years. Trouble was, the reality was better than the dream.

She felt a rush of blood to her cheeks, but Alex had reached across the table and taken her hand.

'Thank you, Ruby. Thank you for doing this for me. Thank you for doing this for my daughter.'

She stood up quickly. *His daughter.*

'It's time to go. I need to get back and plan for the nursery with Annabelle and her nanny.'

He was being kind. He was being sweet. He was thanking her for doing her job.

*Her job.* The one he was paying her to do.

If Alex was disturbed by her abruptness he didn't show it. He just signalled to the waiter and left some money on the table.

Her cheek was burning from where he'd touched her. It almost felt as if he'd left a mark on her skin.

She needed some distance. She needed some space.

Most of all she needed to remember why she was here—to assess a little girl. Nothing more. Nothing less.

# CHAPTER FOUR

FOR A MOMENT earlier today Alex had been sure there was something in the air between him and Ruby.

He'd managed to persuade his security team to stay a comfortable distance away from them. He knew the palace must be suffocating for Ruby. But he'd never considered it might be suffocating to Annabelle.

Ruby was here to do a job. She'd already made an impact on his staff by insisting she stay in the staff quarters next to Annabelle. He'd tried not to smirk when he'd heard Rufus, his private secretary, scold her for calling him Alex.

'You must address him as Your Highness or Prince Regent,' he'd insisted.

But Ruby had laughed and waved her hand. 'Nonsense. He's Alex.'

There was a hum in the air around her. When she remembered, her manners could be impeccable. But most of the time she was just Ruby, and his staff were starting to warm to her.

Her focus on her task was obvious to all. She was unobtrusive, watching Annabelle and listening quietly. None of her assessment had put any demands on the child. After months of people trying to make Annabelle do things she clearly didn't want to, or

examining her ears, tongue and throat, it was a re-
freshing change.

Ruby. She'd been fixed in his mind for the last
ten years. Her brown curls, dark eyes, red coat and
a carefree attitude had wrapped their way around
him like cotton candy around a stick.

But it was other things he remembered too. The
laughter in her eyes, the flirtation, the buzz between
them. That moment when their lips had touched and
the fireworks had started going off in his head as
well as in the sky. Ruby had sent a rush of blood
around his body. He'd never felt a connection like
that. He'd never had a kiss like that again.

He remembered the feel of her warm curves filling the palms of his hand underneath that red coat.
The skin on her cheek where he'd stroked it. Every
sensation of just *being* around Ruby.

Part of what he remembered was reality, part fan-
tasy. He hadn't wanted that night to end. To Ruby,
he'd been just Alex. At that point in his life he'd
been able to do that. But it had been the last night
of his life to have that opportunity, and spending it
with Ruby couldn't have been more perfect. If only
it had ended differently.

He looked down and shuffled the ever-growing
mound of papers on his desk. All things that needed
his signature. Emails were all very well, but some
things still required a signature.

He picked up the phone and dialled the number
of the clinic in Switzerland. It didn't matter that he

knew the doctors would phone him if they had any concerns. Or that he had a multitude of staff members to do it for him. After ten years, he still liked to keep a check of things on his own.

He moved the papers on the desk again, looking to find a letter for a foreign dignitary. Something fluttered to the floor. A photo. He picked it up and smiled. It was ten years old. Ruby, just the way he remembered her, taken by one of his security team on New Year's Eve. He'd only found out about it a few months later, when he'd wanted to track her down. His Head of Security had admitted they had some photographs and had looked into her past—all to check her authenticity.

It was of the two of them, sitting at the table in that café next to the Four Seasons. They were laughing. Ruby had her head thrown back, her dark hair was glossy, and she was smiling from ear to ear. But the thing that had always struck him about that picture was the way they were looking at each other. Even though Ruby was laughing she was still looking at him, and he at her.

A little moment captured in time.

A million different possibilities. A million different futures.

If he'd turned a different corner that night he'd never have met Ruby Wetherspoon, and that thought made his stomach twist almost as much as the thought of what might have been.

Deep down he knew his father would never have

accepted his fascination with an English healthcare worker. He'd never fully understood it himself.

But no one could deny the connection between them. This picture was everlasting proof of that.

When he had his darkest moments—when the nights just seemed to last for ever—it was thoughts of Ruby that gave him comfort. Thoughts of being twenty-four again and having the world at his feet.

He sighed and opened a drawer to put the photo inside. Ruby had never been a threat and his security staff had filed their paperwork away.

He just couldn't do the same.

There it was again. That strange noise.

Ruby moved from the window seat, where she'd been watching the sun start to lower in the sky. Evenings could be long in the palace. Annabelle went to bed early and most of the time Ruby spent her time walking in the gardens, reading a book or talking to Polly on the phone.

Polly was still unimpressed.

The noise again. Was it a whimper?

She stood up quickly. Brigette, the nanny, had gone to bed earlier with a migraine. Could it be Annabelle?

Annabelle's door had been left open earlier, so Ruby walked out into the corridor and hesitated, her hand above the door handle. Part of her was worried. Annabelle wasn't that familiar with her yet. Maybe she would be scared if Ruby went into her room.

She took a deep breath as the whimper continued and pushed the door open. There was no way she could leave any child upset—whether they knew her or not.

The room was dark. Even though the sun hadn't set yet there were blackout blinds at the window. It only took her a few seconds to realise the bed was empty.

She sucked in a breath and suppressed her impulse to shout. Instead she flicked on the light switch and had a quick look around. Annabelle might still be in the room.

But she wasn't. Not under the bed. Not in the wardrobe—even though Ruby hadn't really expected her to be. Not in any corner of the room.

Her heart started thudding as she walked back to the door and quickly along the corridor. The missing child would cause mayhem. The implications were tremendous—and terrifying. She had to take a few seconds to be sure before she called the alarm.

*There.* In front of her. At the top of the stairs.

A tiny staggering figure in pink pyjamas.

Her legs broke into a run.

'Annabelle!'

She reached her seconds.

But Annabelle hadn't responded to her voice. And it was clear why. She was sleepwalking.

Ruby didn't have any experience with sleepwalking kids. She could vaguely remember something about not waking them up. But Annabelle was perilously close to the top of the staircase. She didn't hesitate. She just swept her up into her arms.

Annabelle's eyes were open, and the movement and embrace by Ruby seemed to give her a little start. Her whimpering stopped and she tucked her head into Ruby's neck.

There was no one else about. Not a single person in the corridor.

She hesitated. What next? She walked back along the corridor and paused at Annabelle's door. Her heart was still thudding after that horrible few seconds of thinking something might be wrong.

She couldn't put Annabelle back into her bed and risk it happening again. She'd need to talk to Brigette and Alex in the morning to see if this was normal for Annabelle. No one had mentioned it, and she knew in some kids it was common, but she couldn't risk Annabelle walking near the stairs again.

She walked back into her own room. There was plenty of space in her bed for both of them. At least then she'd know that Annabelle was safe.

Her eyes were still open. Ruby had no idea if it was just an automatic response in sleepwalking, or if on some level Annabelle was actually awake.

The little arms wound around her neck. Thank goodness for automatic reactions. Ruby just started to rock her.

Familiarity. That was what she needed for this little girl.

She kept her in her arms and walked next door, picking up Annabelle's favourite movie and taking it with her.

Background noise. That was all it needed to be. Something familiar so that if Annabelle woke up she'd be comfortable.

Ruby reached her hand out, juggling the weight of Annabelle on the other arm as she opened the case and slid the DVD inside the player.

They settled back on the bed. Annabelle adjusted her position. She seemed comfortable in Ruby's lap and made no attempt to move. Ruby piled the pillows around them. If they were here for the long haul they might as well be comfortable.

The screen lit up bright blue as the titles for *Finding Nemo* appeared. Her own 'go to' film as well as Annabelle's favourite. She loved it just as much as any child, and had yet to meet a kid who wasn't enthralled by it.

Annabelle seemed to settle back against her and that was when Ruby *really* started to listen. She'd already heard Annabelle whimper. She had no doubt that on a physical basis the little girl could form sounds. The diagnosis of selective mutism seemed the most appropriate. She wondered if Annabelle spoke in *any* situation.

She seemed a little more awake now, but she hadn't made any sign to Ruby. Her head was definitely turned towards the TV screen, and she didn't seem to have any objection to being in Ruby's bed.

A new thought crossed her mind, completely unrelated to the sleepwalking. Company. This little girl wanted company.

And then it started. Little noises. Little sounds. Gasps when Nemo's mother disappeared. Small, slow body movements along with the music, and then—eventually—a little hum. Ruby did nothing. She didn't react at all. Just listened as Annabelle hummed along. A smile danced across the little girl's face. She was enthralled—lost in the story. Perfect. Just perfect.

She was only three. Her speech wasn't really too delayed. Maybe Annabelle needed a little encouragement and coaching instead of assessing and prodding. She would have to choose her words carefully when she explained all this to Alex. There was no magic wand that she could wave here. Annabelle had to be allowed to develop at her own pace.

Ruby settled back against the pillows. Annabelle's eyes were getting heavy. She would fall asleep soon—and then Ruby could think about this a little more...

'Ruby!'

Her eyes shot open. The first thing that struck her was the crick in her neck. The second thing that struck her was the three people standing in the doorway—all of them staring at her.

She tried to push herself up, but Annabelle was still curled in her lap, sleeping. Ruby couldn't even begin to imagine what she looked like—rumpled clothes, hair sticking up in every direction but the right one, and more than likely pillow creases on her face.

Brigette, Rufus and Alexander were standing in the doorway, three sets of eyes fixed on her. She tried to edge herself out from under Annabelle without disturbing her. The curtains were still drawn and the TV was flickering on the wall.

Alex rushed across the room. 'What on earth is going on? Why is Annabelle in here?' He seemed furious. 'Have you *any* idea what I thought when I saw her bed was empty?'

He was shouting now, unable to contain his anger.

Of course. The same horrible thought *she'd* had for a few seconds last night, when she'd saw Annabelle's empty bed. The horror. The worry.

She couldn't get the words out quickly enough. 'I'm sorry. I found her sleepwalking last night. She was close to the top of the stairs. I just grabbed her. Then I didn't know whether to try and wake her or not, so I brought her in here. I was worried she might do it again.'

Alex reached over and lifted his still sleeping little girl out of the bed. 'Sleepwalking? Why didn't you call me? Why didn't you call Brigette?'

He was angry with her.

'I'm her father. You should have come and got me if there was something wrong with Annabelle.'

Ruby shook her head. She understood his anger. She understood those seconds of panic.

'There was no one around, Alex. I had no idea if sleepwalking was normal for Annabelle or not. And she seemed to settle with me really quickly. She just wanted some comfort. I did plan to talk to you about it today.'

Alex shot her a look that left her in no doubt about his feelings. He didn't even say another word. Just turned and walked out of the room with Annabelle in his arms, still asleep.

She turned to Brigette. The last thing she wanted to do was get Annabelle's nanny in trouble. 'I'm sorry, Brigette. I knew you had a migraine. I didn't want to wake you when I felt as if I could deal with Annabelle on my own.'

Brigette brushed past her too, leaving Rufus the last person to lock his beady eyes on hers.

She sighed. 'I'm going to take a shower and get dressed.'

Rufus tutted at her and then spun on his heels and left.

*Great. Just great.*

Now she was awake a little more she wanted to shout at them all to come back and tell them to calm down.

Annabelle was fine. They should talk about her sleepwalking and put steps in place to keep her safe.

But common sense told her this wasn't the time.

* * *

He hadn't spoken to Ruby in four days.

It was ridiculous. He'd snapped at her when there had been no reason to. But when Rufus had bustled along the corridor to tell him Annabelle was missing he'd panicked. He could have broken speed records with his bolt along the corridor.

The thought of something happening to his daughter... He couldn't even allow his brain to contemplate it.

But seeing Ruby asleep on the bed with Annabelle in her arms had knocked the wind from his heels.

After the instant relief he'd felt a wave of anger.

Their heads resting next to each other, the mishmash of blonde curls and long brown hair, the way Ruby had been sheltering Annabelle in her arms had consumed him with an unexpected rage he hadn't felt in a long time.

She couldn't know that, against advice, on lots of occasions Sophia had taken Annabelle in to sleep next to her. She could never imagine that the impact of seeing his little girl in someone else's arms would flood him with unspeakable guilt.

He hadn't loved Sophia the way people thought he had. He had loved her like a best friend. A best friend who'd been cheated out of sleeping next to their little girl and seeing her grow up.

If Sophia was here now he was almost sure Annabelle wouldn't have any problems with her speech.

As for the sleepwalking…? Was that his fault too? It was yet another worry. Another failing. Something else to consult a whole array of doctors on.

He couldn't even begin to understand why it annoyed him all the more that it was Ruby who'd found the problem. She was under his skin in more ways than was imaginable.

Guilt was chipping away at him. Guilt for how he was feeling about Ruby. And guilt because he continually felt as if he were failing his daughter.

What would Sophia have thought? His friend would have dealt with things so much better than he could.

But if Sophia were here now he would never have seen Ruby again. And that was what burned away at his insides. That was what filled him with even more hideous guilt.

The last few days of being around Ruby had lit a fire inside him that had long since died. He could feel her presence everywhere. The staff in the palace seemed happier—less formal. It was almost as if her scent drifted in the air into every room. Light, flowery, lifting the mood.

She'd connected with most members of staff in her polite but informal manner. She wasn't afraid to ask questions, and more importantly she wasn't afraid to laugh. In the space of a few days the atmosphere around him seemed to have lightened. The palace had started to feel happy again.

Years of worry about his father's health, the economy of Euronia, and then the terminal diagnosis of Sophia, followed by the concerns about Annabelle, had made being here oppressive. Every tiny part of this place seemed to weigh on his shoulders relentlessly.

Seeing Ruby's connection today with Annabelle had been unexpected. He'd never realistically thought about someone else stepping into Sophia's shoes.

But he should have. It was inevitable.

At some point he would marry again—this time for love—and that woman would become a mother to Annabelle. He'd been so busy these last few years, and so stressed, he hadn't taken time to think of the impact of that.

The impact on the country. The impact on Annabelle. The impact on him.

And then, there she was, with her mussed-up curls parallel with his child's. Making him see something that everyone had probably already surmised.

It was time to move on.

But was he ready?

# CHAPTER FIVE

THE CLOTHES WERE lying across her bed. Seventeen dresses of varying styles and colours—all with matching shoes.

'I don't understand. Did something happen to my clothes?'

Rufus shook his head. 'I told you I would arrange for some other clothing to be sent to the palace for you.'

She reached down and touched the nearest designer dress. It was red...beautiful. Like something you would wear to the Queen's garden party back in London. It certainly wasn't like anything she owned.

'But I'm not sure I really need these. I don't know how much longer I'll be here. And I've got clothes of my own.' She opened the wardrobe, revealing her few dresses, jeans, T-shirts and a couple of pairs of sandals and heels.

Rufus gave an almost imperceptible shake of his head. He turned to leave. 'They're here now— enjoy!' he said, and with a wave of his hand he disappeared, leaving her to perch on the edge of the bed, too nervous to touch some of the dresses.

'How very *Pretty Woman*.' She sighed. Her head

was swimming. Was this another way for Alex to buy her? Did he want to dress her up like some doll?

Every dress was beautifully styled and there was a rainbow of colour. It was strange, but whilst they were all different none was in a style that she wouldn't wear. It was almost as if they'd given her friend Polly a free budget and the run of all the designer houses.

A silk one slid through her fingers. It was almost the same blue as Alex's eyes. She gave a little shudder.

Alex. He hadn't spoken to her for four days. Falling asleep with his daughter was obviously a no-no. But while it might have been a little unconventional she really thought everyone had overreacted.

The imaginary walls between herself and Annabelle had definitely started to crumble. The little girl wasn't completely ignoring her any more. Yesterday she'd sat next to Ruby as she'd thumbed through a book. After a while Ruby had asked her if she wanted her to read the story and Annabelle had given a little nod and slid closer.

It was a small step, but gaining Annabelle's trust was the most important thing of all.

She picked up another of the dresses. It was yellow—a colour she never usually wore—and it matched the sun outside and the flowers in the garden directly beneath her window.

She slipped off her T-shirt and Capri pants. The dress dropped over her head and fitted her curves as if it had been specially made for her. Everything was covered, from the round neckline to the flouncy skirt that fell to her knees. She reached behind to fasten the zip. It was a little tricky. She managed to pull it up to her bra strap. Then she reached her hands above her shoulders and over her back, trying to pull the material of the dress a little higher and grasp the zipper.

Someone cleared his throat loudly. She spun around.

She hadn't thought to close the door after Rufus had left. No one ever seemed to come down this corridor.

'Alex!' Colour flooded into her cheeks.

He was leaning in the doorway, his hands folded across his chest, with a cheeky smile on his face. She hadn't even heard his footsteps.

'What are you doing here?'

His smile just seemed to get broader. 'Looks like I'm helping a damsel in distress.' He stepped into the room and twirled his finger. 'Go on—spin around and I'll fasten it for you.'

It was amazing how quickly his presence could cause a buzz in the air around her. She sucked in a breath as she turned around.

Fastening a zip should take the briefest of seconds. But Alex waited. She could feel the material of her dress shifting slightly. The zipper must be in his hand. Then he stepped forward, closing the gap between them.

His head was at her shoulder. She could smell his aftershave—it was coiling its way around her. Who was the snake in that childhood film? Kaa, in *The Jungle Book*—with the hypnotic eyes that could make you do anything that he wanted. She was pretty sure Alex's eyes would have the same effect on her.

'I'm sorry I snapped at you,' he said quietly. 'I thought something was wrong with Annabelle.'

'Okay…' That was all she replied. Her breath was still caught somewhere between her chest and her throat. It was all she was capable of saying right now.

There was a drumming noise in her ears. Her heart was thudding against her chest as she waited to see what would happen next.

'I thought today we could go back to the café with Annabelle—like you asked me to.'

She smiled. Did that mean her mistake was being forgotten, or was this part of his apology? He still hadn't moved. He still hadn't fastened her zipper.

She nodded. Not breathing was getting difficult. 'Okay.'

'Do you like the dresses?'

She could feel his breath warm the skin on her shoulder.

'I love them—but I don't need them. Rufus didn't need to do that.'

'He didn't do it.'

She froze. One of his hands moved and rested on her hip.

This was all becoming remarkably familiar. Richard Gere was going to appear any second now. Didn't he buy Vivian a new wardrobe in *Pretty Woman*?

Her profession might not compare with Vivian's, but the thought of Alex purchasing a whole wardrobe for her was both mildly disturbing and somehow exciting. She didn't know whether to be insulted or overjoyed.

'I don't think I like this, Alex. You can't buy me. You can't dress me up as if I'm your little doll.' She could feel her stomach tighten.

But Alex just shook his head. 'I'm not buying you, Ruby. I don't care whether you wear the clothes or not.' He waved his hand. 'If you don't like them give them away—give them to charity. It makes no difference to me.'

He stepped a little closer.

'I guess I'm just not good at this. I'm trying to say sorry. Sorry about how I reacted over Annabelle. For a second I thought she was gone. I thought someone had kidnapped my daughter—I overreacted. And…' He waved his hands again. 'This is how I say sorry. Doesn't every woman like clothes?'

The tightness in her chest dissipated. It was clear he meant every word.

'What are you going to do if it happens again?'

He smiled. 'Silent alarms. Everywhere. If Annabelle opens her door in the middle of the night alarms will go off in my room, Brigette's room and in Security.' He looked over his shoulder and whispered. 'And, don't tell her, but we've actually had tracking devices sewn into all her pyjamas.'

She laughed. He was sorry, and he'd put steps in place to ensure Annabelle's safety. Of course he had. She hadn't doubted that for a second, but it made her mood lighten.

He nudged her, and pointed to the dresses as he slid a hand around her waist.

'Which is your favourite?'

He was so close. His lips were almost touching her ear. If she just moved her head a little…

'The blue one.'

'Why?'

'I like the colour.' The rush of blood was heating her cheeks. Her answer had been automatic.

She was conscious of the lightness of his fingers on her hip. Would he make the connection between the colour of the dress and the colour of his eyes? No. Guys didn't do that kind of thing.

This time his lips did brush against her ear. 'I like the red one. It reminds me of you in Paris. The same colour as your coat.'

A whole host of tiny centipedes were marching along her arms with their hundreds of legs, making every single hair stand on end.

His finger touched the skin of her back. She gasped. It wasn't cold—it was just unexpected. A thousand butterfly wings had just exploded on her back, and all the little nerve-endings were waiting for the next sensation.

He bent a little lower and whispered in her ear again. This time it felt as if his breath was caressing her skin.

'Ten years is a long time, Ruby.'

He pulled the zipper up with his finger inside, then ran it along the upper end of her spine, resting his fingers at the base of her neck.

Her legs were turning to jelly. It was ridiculous. It was nothing. But she felt as if she'd waited ten years for that.

Ten years of dreaming. Ten years of imagining. Ten years of hoping.

She stepped backwards. Against him. Into him. Feeling the full length of his body next to hers. Her eyes were fixed outside, on the gardens. If she turned around and looked at those blue eyes she might do something much more inappropriate than fall asleep next to his daughter.

She rested her head back against his chest. 'Yes, it is.'

Her voice was tinged with sadness.

They both stood there—neither moving. It was almost as if they were happy for this to be the first tiny step. The first real acknowledgment that their time ten years ago hadn't just been a figment of her imagination that she'd played over and over in her head.

She could feel the rise and fall of his chest against her back. The heat from his body through the thin fabric of her dress. It felt natural. It felt as if this was exactly the place she was supposed to stand. As if this was exactly the place she was meant to be.

His hand moved slightly from her hip around to her stomach. His other hand met hers and he threaded their fingers together in front of her.

This might be wrong.

It might be inappropriate.

But why did it feel so good?

'Your Highness?'

The voice came echoing down the hall and they sprang apart. Alex disappeared out of her door in flash to meet Rufus, who was muttering again.

Ruby's feet were stuck to the floor.

Had that really just happened?

Her body was telling her yes. Every sense seemed to be on fire.

But her brain was turning to mush. Sensible, rational thoughts seemed to have flown from the building.

Ruby was logical. Ruby was always sensible.

The one time in her life she hadn't been entirely sensible had been ten years ago in Paris. Ten years ago she'd acted on impulse. And look where that had got her.

But ten years ago she'd felt the same tiny flicker of warmth and excitement that was burning inside her right now.

This was the first time she hadn't felt like the hired help.

This was the first time she'd felt as if she wasn't here just for Annabelle.

Question was: what was she getting herself into?

# CHAPTER SIX

ALEX'S HANDS WERE still shaking. That had been it. The situation that—in his head—he'd dreamed about being in.

Him and Ruby alone.

Getting private time in the palace was harder than it seemed.

Ruby's questions a few days ago had started to play on his mind. How much time *did* he actually get to spend with Annabelle?

He tried to be there most mornings when she had breakfast. He always tried to see her before bedtime. But in a world where visits to other countries were inevitable and midnight conference calls were normal it wasn't always possible.

Annabelle was the spitting image of her mother. He'd already been friends with Sophia at her age. And, although he loved his daughter with all his heart, sometimes she was a painful reminder of the friend he had lost.

Perhaps he'd overreacted when the nanny had mentioned Annabelle's speech seemed a little behind?

Alex had no experience with children. And the internet seemed like a dangerous tool sometimes. He'd paid for expert upon expert to assess her—all the while terrified that there was something wrong with his child.

When Ruby had said that as part of the assessment she wanted to see how Annabelle and Alex interacted with each other he'd felt a wave of panic. Was it a criticism? She hadn't made it sound like that. Maybe he was just feeling under pressure.

He'd planned carefully. He'd had someone pack a picnic to take to the palace grounds, then they would walk into the centre and have some ice cream—just as Ruby had suggested.

Then he gone to find Ruby and she'd been surrounded by the dresses he'd ordered and been half dressed.

Maybe not strictly true. But that glimpse of the skin on her back had been enough to send his blood pressure rising. When he'd offered to zip her up it had taken all his strength not to pull the zip down.

Alex was always in control. That night in Paris years ago had been the first time he'd shaken off his security team in years. Bumping into Ruby had made the whole night perfect. Having her in the palace again was bringing a whole host of sensations he hadn't acknowledged in years.

Rufus had mumbled in his ear all the way along the corridor. The look of surprise on his face to see Alex exiting Ruby's bedroom had spoken volumes without a single word being said.

Neither of them had acknowledged it. Alex had immediately started talking business and given

Rufus a list of instructions for the rest of the afternoon.

Annabelle and her nanny were waiting at the main entrance for him. After a few minutes Ruby came down the main staircase carrying a bright pink ball in her arms. Her face was slightly flushed. A sure sign they'd been doing something they shouldn't.

Brigette gave a nod and left while Alex offered his hand to Annabelle and put the picnic basket over his arm.

'A picnic? You never said we were having a picnic,' said Ruby.

'Didn't I?'

He glanced at the ball, then at her feet. She was wearing a pair of white trainers with a yellow dress. It brought a smile to his face. Ruby didn't really worry about who might take her picture and claim she'd made a fashion *faux pas*.

'I didn't take you as a footballer.'

Ruby pulled at the skirt of her dress and smiled. 'I have lots of hidden talents. But maybe I should have worn something different—trousers, perhaps?'

He shook his head. 'I think your dress will be perfect. Now, let's go.'

There was a further little flush of colour in her cheeks. Both of them were remembering exactly why he liked the fact she was wearing a dress.

But Ruby wasn't giving anything away. She bent down in front of Annabelle. 'A picnic—wow. It's been years since I've been on a picnic. Why don't you take us to your favourite place in the palace grounds and we'll eat there?'

She gave Alex a little smile and walked out through the door, waiting for them to join her.

He could sense the general unease in the air. There were a few members of staff staring at them. Was it really so unusual that he spent time with his child—or had word spread even more quickly than he'd thought that he'd been seen leaving Ruby's bedroom?

He gave Annabelle's hand a squeeze and they walked out into the beautiful sunshine. Ruby's idea was good. He'd been trying to decide between going near where the horses were stabled, to the ornamental gardens, the duck pond or the palace maze. But Annabelle had other ideas. She was leading them around the side of the palace, her little footsteps assured.

It only took a few minutes, then she plunked herself down on the grass directly behind the ornamental fountain.

Alex blinked. This was the place where he'd had that picture taken with Sophia. They'd both been about Annabelle's page and the photo had been zoomed around the world with the press headline *'Future King and Queen?'*

Had Annabelle ever seen that picture? He wasn't sure, but he could tell from a fleeting glance at Ruby's face that *she* certainly had.

Whatever her thoughts on the matter, she sat

down next to Annabelle on the grass, not even waiting for him to lay out the picnic blanket he'd brought along.

The little girl started to fumble with her shoes. Ruby gave her a smile and knelt down next to her, taking off her white leather sandals and frilly socks.

She held out her hand to Annabelle and the two of them walked over to the fountain. Annabelle hadn't said a word and he was confused. How did Ruby know what she wanted?

He moved closer as Annabelle stood up on the wall surrounding the fountain and dipped her toes in the water. She let out a little laugh and he took a deep breath.

His little girl's laughter. How beautiful it was— and how rarely he'd heard it.

Annabelle was walking around the fountain now, holding Ruby's hand to keep her balance. She had the biggest smile on her face.

He walked in pace with Ruby. 'How did you know that's what she wanted to do?'

He couldn't take his eyes off his little girl. Couldn't believe how much she looked like her mother. It alarmed him how much he noticed.

Ruby shrugged. 'It's exactly what I would do if I were Annabelle's age.'

They reached the point where they'd started and Ruby put her arms around Annabelle's waist and swung her in the air.

'Whee!'

Annabelle laughed again as Ruby swooped her through the air and landed her on the blanket that he'd spread out. She picked up a corner of the blanket and started drying Annabelle's toes.

Alex opened the basket and started unpacking the food. The palace chef had outdone himself, as usual, but the most curious thing was a small tub full of steamed-up food.

Annabelle gave a little shriek of excitement and grabbed it, pulling open the lid and searching for a spoon.

Ruby wrinkled her nose and leaned closer. 'Macaroni cheese? Is this one of Annabelle's favourites?'

Alex nodded. 'Apparently.' He peered in the basket. 'I'm not quite sure how it managed to find its way into the picnic basket, though.'

Ruby grabbed an apple, bit into it, then leaned back on her hands, staring up at the palace. 'I can't say I've ever had a picnic in front of a palace before.'

He stared up at the hundreds of windows. There might be a whole host of palace staff looking down on them at any moment. It might look like a private picnic, with no one visibly around them, but the truth was it was anything but.

He pulled a bottle of water out of the basket and popped the tab for Annabelle. 'Would you like to go and see the horses? Or the maze?'

She shook her head and continued to eat the macaroni. He reached into the basket for some more food, and squinted when his hand came into contact with something strange. A leg. A plastic doll's leg. And another doll. And another.

He pulled them out. One was in a princess dress, one in a swimsuit and one in a semi-naked state with her arms partway into a spacesuit.

He winked at Ruby. 'Ruby, I see you brought your dolls to play with.'

She laughed and grabbed the blonde astronaut, pushing her arms and legs into the silver and white suit and fastening it appropriately. 'Of course I did, Alex. I like playing with dolls.'

Annabelle's head shot up and she gave a little smile, abandoning the macaroni and walking over to the dolls. Her comprehension was perfect. She understood everything that was going on around her. So why didn't she talk?

Ruby held up the princess doll and the swimsuit doll. 'Which one do you like best? The pink one or the purple one?'

He wondered what she was doing. Annabelle screwed up her face and shook her head. There were no pink or purple clothes.

Ruby just smiled, as if this was something she did every day—which she did. She held each doll higher. 'Oh, I *see*. Silly me. Blue or red, then?'

Annabelle came over and picked the doll wearing the pale blue dress and pointed towards her own.

Ruby nodded. 'You like blue, then?'

She gave Alex a secret smile. Every little thing she did was part of Annabelle's assessment. Every other person who had come to see her had been much more rigid in their processes, wanting Annabelle to do certain things at certain times. Being three was difficult enough. But Alex had been made to feel as if Annabelle was being difficult or uncooperative. She didn't seem that way with Ruby.

Annabelle took her dolls and walked over to the ornamental fountain with all three.

'I think they're all about to go for a swim—costumes or not,' murmured Ruby.

She seemed perfectly relaxed out here. She picked up a ham sandwich and started to eat. He reached in and pulled out his favourite. Tuna. Hardly royal. Probably not the thing that most Prince Regents would eat. But this had been Alex's favourite since he was a child.

The tension between them wasn't as high as it had been in the room when they were alone. But then again, they hadn't been on display there. He kept wondering if there *were* any unseen eyes watching what should be a private affair.

'She knows her colours. For a three-year-old that's good.' Ruby was watching Annabelle again.

'You can tell just from that?'

She shook her head. 'Oh, no. I've done a few other exercises as well.' She leaned forward and pulled her knees up, wrapping her dress around them. 'Listen…' she whispered.

Alex sat a little straighter, straining to hear what

Ruby had heard above the constant trickle of water from the fountain.

There it was—floating across the air.

Ruby touched his arm. 'She's humming. She did that the other night with me.' She gave a tiny shake of her head. 'I know that one of the reports about Annabelle questioned whether she could even make sounds. But she can. You've heard her laugh. You've heard her squeal. And she can communicate with sign language. She's *choosing* not to speak.' A frown marred her complexion. 'I've just got to figure out why.'

Her eyes were fixed on Annabelle playing with her dolls. This was all so easy for Ruby. Annabelle was just a patient. She didn't have the same investment, the same emotional connection that he did. She didn't have the same frustrated feeling that there must be something else he could do. She was a professional with a puzzle to solve.

'You make it sound so easy.' He couldn't help the way the words sounded. He'd forced them out through gritted teeth.

But Ruby didn't react. She just kept looking at Annabelle. 'I don't think it's easy, Alex. I just think that you—and I—are going to have to be patient. That's the only way this can work.'

Her eyes met his. For a second he wasn't quite sure what she was talking about. They were talking about Annabelle, right? Because those words might sound as if she were talking about them instead.

'What's your first memory, Alex?'

'What?' He was surprised by her question.

She smiled at him. 'I can honestly say the first thing I remember is from around age seven. I was on holiday with my mum and dad in Boulogne in France. I can remember walking about with cases because we couldn't find our hotel. Then my father thought it would be interesting to go and watch the fishermen.' She gave a shudder. 'Watching fishermen gut their fish was not something I wanted to see as a seven-year-old.' She turned and smiled at him. 'That's my first real memory.'

He sat back a little, unsure where this was going. 'I can remember having to sit very still for a long, *long* time. It was at some awards ceremony and my father glared at me every time I moved. I hated the shirt and tie I was wearing because it felt too tight.'

She nodded. 'What age do you think you were?'

He shrugged. 'Around five, I think.'

She lifted her hand towards Annabelle. 'Here's the thing. Science tells us that the first three years are the most important for a child's brain development. It's the first time we're supposed to form memories—but I can't remember anything from back then. The experts tell us that young children's memories change over time, replacing old memories with new ones. So I'm looking at Annabelle and wondering what she remembers.'

'What do you mean?' This was starting to make him uncomfortable.

She interlinked her fingers. 'The brain has connections—hard wiring. Children's brains are like a sponge—they take in everything all around them. Children are born to learn. By their first year seventy-five per cent of the hard wiring is in place.' She pointed at Annabelle again. 'By age three ninety per cent of the hard wiring is there.'

She ran her fingers through her hair.

'Under the age of two, lots of their development depends on attachment. I wonder if Annabelle's speech issues could actually be down to the loss of her mother.'

'What?' Alex shook his head. It was something he hadn't even considered. 'But she was only eleven months old when Sophia died.'

Ruby nodded slowly, 'Exactly. A baby recognises its mother's voice in the womb. Once it's born it puts the face and voice together. It responds to those. You said that Sophia was a good mother and spent most of her time with Annabelle?'

He nodded. 'Yes, she did.'

'Then for eleven months Annabelle's hard wiring was formed all around her mother.'

Ruby sat back, letting what she'd said sink around him. She seemed to know when she'd said enough.

She wasn't apportioning any blame. She wasn't being confrontational. She was being logical. She was giving him information and letting him think for himself what it might mean.

He sat quietly. Ruby was relaxed and Annabelle

seemed happy. She was busy trying to drown all her plastic dolls in the ornamental fountain and probably block the pumps from here to eternity.

No matter what Ruby had just told him it was comfortable. It was relaxed.

The sandwiches disappeared quickly, followed by some little cakes at the bottom of the picnic basket. Ruby didn't feel the need to chatter and fill the silence. She was entirely happy to lie back on the blanket and watch Annabelle.

This was something he never got time to do any more.

There was always something to be signed, someone who needed to talk to him urgently. An email or a letter to write. A dignitary to entertain. A celebrity to pander to in order to bring extra publicity and business to Euronia.

Where was the time for Annabelle in all that?

Where was the time for him?

He never got time to be just a father. He never got time to be just Alex. Did anyone in the palace even think of him as just Alex?

He watched as Ruby moved, crawling on all fours, ignoring her dress and bare knees, creeping across the red stones to meet Annabelle and start splashing her with water from the fountain.

Annabelle shrieked in delight and ran around the fountain. It was the finest sound he'd ever heard.

Two minutes later Ruby had the pink plastic ball and was throwing it over the top of the fountain to

Annabelle at the other side. But that was soon too safe—too ordinary. Within a few seconds they'd both climbed on the wall at each side of the fountain and were throwing the ball to each other while balancing precariously on the low wall.

He should intervene. He should tell them to stop being so silly. Last time they'd had to replace the blue tiles in the wall of the fountain it had taken for ever. He couldn't even remember the cost.

But both of them were laughing out loud. He couldn't remember the last time he'd seen Annabelle so happy. And it was Ruby who was responsible for that.

Something twisted inside him. Part of it was pride, part of it a little inkling of jealousy. Deep down he knew that *he* should be the one making his little girl laugh like that. But if it couldn't be him he was so glad that it was Ruby.

Ruby was genuine. Ruby related to his daughter in a way that none of the other professionals had.

He had been so right to bring her here.

Even when the palace officials had voiced their obvious concerns about his latest plans to get Annabelle assessed he'd known that this was the right thing to do.

He'd been right to remember the passion in her eyes when she'd spoken about missing out on the job she would have loved. He'd followed her for years...sent her unsigned flowers. He remembered his surge of pride when he'd found out she'd got her dream job, when she'd been promoted, when she'd published professional papers. All those things had made him happy for her.

Now, in a few short days, she'd started to connect with his daughter.

With him.

There was a scream, followed by a huge splash. A flash of moving yellow rushed before his eyes. He was on his feet instantly.

Annabelle's eyes were wide. She jumped down from her side of the fountain and ran around it towards the splash, meeting her father as they both peered down into the few feet of clear water.

Ruby was completely under the water, tiny bubbles snaking out from her mouth, her yellow dress billowing around her. Alex leaned over to put his hand in and pull her up—then gasped as she opened her eyes.

The expression on her face was priceless. Annabelle dissolved into fits of laughter as Ruby burst up through the surface of the water, shrieking with laughter.

Alex's eyes shot up towards the hundreds of windows of the palace. He could only imagine what anyone on his staff might say if they'd witnessed this.

But the laughter was infectious. And Ruby wasn't at all worried about the fact that her hair was sodden and she was soaked to the skin.

She reached towards his outstretched arm,

smiled, and tugged sharply—pulling him straight in next to her.

Even though the sun was shining the water in the fountain was freezing.

His landing was partly cushioned by the soft body of Ruby. Water was dripping from the end of her nose, her hair was flattened to her head and her clothes hugged every part of her body.

'Who are you laughing at?' She winked.

He couldn't do anything other than laugh. Annabelle was still jumping up and down at the side of the fountain.

Ruby reached down and picked up a submerged princess doll. 'I came in to rescue the doll—what's your excuse?'

He smiled, their faces only inches apart. He lifted his eyebrows, 'Oh, I definitely came in to rescue Ruby.'

His arms were on either side of her, his chin just above her head. Every part of him was soaked.

'Who says I needed rescuing?' she quipped.

She didn't care. She didn't care about her wet clothes or how she looked. She wasn't constantly looking over her shoulder for a camera. Ruby was just Ruby.

And it was at that moment that he realised. Realised this was bigger than he ever could have imagined.

Every thought, every memory of this fountain had been imprinted on his brain for thirty-four years. That famous photo had been shared firstly in the newspapers, and later around the world on the internet.

Every single time he'd looked at this fountain it had brought back memories of Sophia and their childhood. He could clearly remember sitting on the edge of the fountain with her, banging his heels on the stonework.

But now, and for ever, every time he looked at this fountain this was what he'd remember. *This*. A water-soaked, laughing Ruby with a twinkle in her eyes and a bright-eyed little girl watching at the side.

Some memories were worth changing.

# CHAPTER SEVEN

THERE WAS DEFINITELY something wrong with her. She was getting used to these clothes. She was getting used to opening the closet and seeing the rainbow colours of the beautiful garments hanging up and just waiting to be worn.

Her blue jeans had been stuffed in the back of the cupboard, along with her baseball boots. It had only been two weeks and she didn't even want to pull them out any more.

Even the pale green dress that she'd worn when she'd arrived—the best thing she had—looked like a poor cousin hanging beside all the designer clothes.

It made her skin prickle. She'd never been like this before. Every girl liked nice things. But she hadn't expected to get used to it so suddenly.

What would happen in a few weeks, when she was back in London, in her flat, wearing her healthcare uniform again? She'd always worn that uniform with pride. What on earth was happening to her?

Alex had been keeping to his side of the bargain and spending a certain amount of time with Annabelle. She'd been trying not to interfere—no matter how much she wanted to.

It was important that there was time for just father and daughter. But the rest of the palace staff didn't seem to understand that. She'd had no idea how busy Alex really was. It seemed that a country/principality didn't run itself.

After watching the constant interruptions of their father/daughter time she'd appointed herself guardian of that little part of the day. She'd started to stand guard outside the door.

By the time Annabelle was settled into her bed and he'd read a few stories to her there was usually a queue of people standing outside the bedroom, waiting to see Alex. Not one of them ever got past her.

The hard wiring talk seemed to have done the trick. It had given him the gentle kick up the backside he needed to say no to people who weren't his daughter. It was sad, but clear, that Alex hadn't been able to spend as much time with Annabelle as he would have liked.

Now he made it his priority. And Ruby's role was to make sure that father and daughter got that protected time together.

'Knock-knock.'

The voice made her jump. She was sitting in the palace library, looking out over the gardens.

This had quickly become her favourite room. The beautiful wood and paper smell crept along the corridor towards her and drew her in like a magnet. The dark wooden bookcases filled with beautiful hardback books seemed to suck her in every time she walked past. The set of steps that moved on a rail to reach the books at the top almost made her jump up and down with excitement. Every time she entered the room she climbed a few steps and moved them on just a little.

She'd even taken to bringing her computer down here and answering any emails she received from work in her favourite environment. She needed to stay in touch with her colleagues to make sure things were running smoothly back home. There were only a few emails each day—mainly about patients, asking for a second opinion or a referral route for a patient with unusual conditions. Nothing she couldn't handle from thousands of miles away.

She spun around in her chair. 'Alex? Is something wrong?'

He smiled. 'Do I only come and look for you if something is wrong?'

She leaned her elbow on the desk and rested her head on the heel of her hand. 'Let's see—maybe?'

She was teasing him. Sometimes he made it so easy. But most things were easy around Alex—except for the times when he was surrounded by palace staff. She could almost swear that Rufus stalked him from one end of the palace to the other.

'Well, let's change that. You've been here for a few weeks now, and apart from the palace grounds and a few walks into the city centre you've hardly seen anything of Euronia. How about we remedy that?'

He held his hand out towards her. She hesitated. Since the dress incident and the day at the fountain something had changed between them. It was happening slowly. Almost without her even noticing. But the way Alex looked at her was different.

Sometimes she caught him staring with the blue eyes of a man ten years younger, without the responsibilities of today on his shoulders. Those were her favourite moments.

Ten years of thinking about 'what ifs'... It was easy to pretend that she hadn't. That she'd been busy with work and life and relationships. But underneath all that there had always been something simmering beneath the surface.

Her first sight of him in her hospital department had knocked the breath from her lungs—not that she'd ever admit that. She had a hard time even admitting it to herself.

In her mind, Ruby Wetherspoon had never been that kind of girl. Dreaming of princes and happy-ever-afters. But her brain kept trying to interfere with her rational thoughts. It kept giving her secret flashes of holding hands, or more kisses. It kept making her imagine what might have happened on the rest of that night on New Year's Eve.

But there was no point dreaming of the past. Today was about looking to the future.

She was beginning to feel a glimmer of hope that there could *be* a future. Her confidence around Alex was starting to grow.

She stood up. The only 'what ifs' were for the here and now.

She reached out and took his hand, his warm skin enveloping hers. 'Where do you plan on taking me?' She looked down, 'And am I suitably dressed?'

He grinned. 'You might need alternative clothes.'

'Really? Why?'

He winked. 'You'll see.'

If the crew were surprised to see him accompanied by a lady they did their best to hide it. It had been a few months since he'd been out on the yacht, and in the past he'd always gone alone.

He hadn't even mentioned the yacht to Ruby, and her face had been a picture as they'd walked onto the dock.

She'd blinked at the gleaming white yacht. It was made of steel and over three hundred feet long.

He waved his arm, 'Ruby, I'd like you to meet the other woman in my life—the *Augusta*.'

'She's huge.' She could see all the staff on board. This wasn't a one-man sailing boat.

He nodded and headed over to the gangway. 'Five bedrooms and an owner's stateroom with living room, bedroom, bathroom and veranda. She's pretty much a guy's dream come true.'

Her foot hesitated at the gangway. His heart gave a little twist. He hadn't even asked her if she was afraid of water. *Please don't let this be a disaster*. He'd already arranged for some swimming and snorkelling gear to be dropped off at the yacht.

But her hesitation was momentary and she steadied her balance on the swaying gangway by holding on to the rail.

'Shouldn't a boat have sails?' she whispered as they walked over the gangway.

'It's a yacht. And it doesn't need sails—it's got four diesel engines. It can probably go faster than some cars.'

She grinned and stopped mid-step, 'Well, aren't *we* a bit snippy about our boat?' She was clearly amused by his automatic response.

He wrinkled his nose. 'Snippy? What does that mean?'

She stepped a little closer. She'd changed into a pale blue dress and flat sandals. He could see the tiny freckles across the bridge of her nose and feel her scent invade his senses. It didn't matter that the smell of the Mediterranean Sea was all around them. The only thing he could concentrate on right now was the smell of some kind of flowers, winding its way around him.

'It means you don't like anyone calling your yacht a boat.' She waved her hand. 'Boat, ship, yacht—it's all the same to me.'

He laughed and shook his head. 'What's that word you use in the UK? Landlubber?'

She nodded as he guided her up on to the deck. 'I'll wear that badge with pride. I know absolutely nothing about sailing. The only boats I've ever sailed were the ones in my bath tub.'

There it was—that little twinkle in her eye. It

happened whenever they joked together, whenever Ruby was relaxed and there was no one else around but them. He didn't see it often enough.

She settled into one of the white chairs as the yacht moved smoothly out from the port. The sea could be choppy around Euronia, but today it was calm.

His steward appeared. 'What would you like for lunch, Ms. Wetherspoon? The chef will make whatever you desire.'

He saw her visibly blanch. There were so many things he took for granted. At any time in the palace he could ask for whatever he wanted to eat. There was always staff available to cater to his tastes. Ruby looked almost embarrassed by the question.

'I guess since I'm on the sea it should be some kind of fish.' She shot the steward a beaming smile. 'What would you suggest?'

If the steward was surprised by her question he didn't show it. 'We have crayfish, mussels, clams and oysters. Or, if you prefer we have sardines— or bouillabaisse. It's a fish stew, practically our national dish.'

'That sounds lovely. I'll have that, thank you.'

The yacht was working its way along the coastline. Within a few minutes the pink palace came into view.

Ruby stood up. 'Wow! It looks so different, seeing it from the sea. It really does look like something from a little girl's toybox. It's gorgeous.'

Alex rolled his eyes. 'You can imagine how I felt as a teenager, living in a pink palace.'

She smiled. Her eyes were still sparkling. 'I *can* imagine. But look at it. It's impressive enough when you see it on land—but from here...? It's like something from a fairytale.'

'What's your favourite room?'

'In the palace?'

He nodded.

The steward had brought some champagne and an ice bucket and Alex popped the cork and started pouring the champagne into glasses.

She took a sip from the glass he handed her. 'It has to be the library. It's the smell. I love it. I could sit in there all day.'

'That was my mother's favourite room too. She was always in the library.'

Ruby turned to face him. 'You don't really talk about your mother. What was she like? I've seen some photographs. She was beautiful.'

He nodded. 'Yes, she was. Most people talk about the clothes she wore and her sense of style. Marguerite de Castellane was known the world over for her beautiful wardrobe. But I remember my mother as having a really wicked sense of humour. And she was clever. She spoke four languages and brought me up speaking both English and French. She died from a clot in her lung—a pulmonary embolism. She'd had the flu and been off her feet for a few weeks. Her legs were swollen and sore—but she didn't tell anyone until it was too late.'

He couldn't help but feel a wave of sadness as he spoke about his mother. To everyone else she had been the Queen. But to an only child with an almost absent father his mother had been his whole world.

She'd kept him grounded. She'd made sure he attended the local school and the local nursery. She'd sent him shopping for bread at the bakers and meat at the delicatessen. Everything he'd learned about being a 'normal' person he'd learned from his mother.

His father had aged twenty years after she'd died. Still working, still ruling his country, but his heart hadn't been in it.

The relationship between father and son had always been strained. And it hadn't improved with age or with his father's ill health.

Ruby had little lines across her forehead now. Even when she frowned she still looked good. He felt a surge of emotion towards her.

He didn't talk to *anyone* about his mother. In years gone by he had spoken to Sophia, but that had been like talking to a friend. Ruby hadn't known his mother. She would only have whatever had been posted on the internet to refer to.

It felt good to share. She made it so easy to talk.

With her legs stretched out in front of her, sipping champagne from the glass, she looked right at home. But he knew she wasn't.

She might be comfortable around him, but she wasn't comfortable around the palace. The formalities of palace life were difficult for her.

She didn't ask or expect anyone to do things for her. Rufus had already mentioned how she'd ruffled some feathers by trying to do her own laundry or make her own toast.

'What about your family?'

She smiled. 'My mum and dad are both just about to retire. They've already told me they plan to move to the South of France. They bought a house there last month. They've holidayed there for the last ten years and have really got into the way of life.'

'Have they ever been to Euronia?'

She rolled her eyes and took another sip of champagne, holding the glass up towards him. 'Only billionaires come to Euronia, Alex.'

He was instantly defensive. 'That's not true. There are cruise ships moored every day in port, and we have bus tours that come across the border from France—'

'Alex.'

She leaned over and touched his arm. The palm of her hand was cool from holding the champagne glass.

'I was teasing.'

The smile reached right up into her eyes and he wrapped his hand over hers.

'Sometimes I'm just not sure.' He stayed exactly where he was. His eyes fixed on hers.

She wasn't shy. She didn't tear her gaze away. Her lips were turned upwards, but as he looked at her more closely her smile seemed a little sad.

'What do you think would have happened between us, Ruby?'

He didn't need to fill in the blanks. She knew exactly what he was talking about. He saw her take a careful breath in.

'I have no idea, Alex,' she whispered. 'Sometimes I've thought about it—thought about what might have happened if things had been different. But neither of us know. Neither of us can really imagine. Ten years changes a person. I'm not the girl I was in Paris, and you're not the boy.'

He nodded his head and grinned at her. 'You thought I was a *boy*?'

Now he was teasing. But she was right. They could spend hours talking about what might have been but it wouldn't do either of them any good. He'd spent too long thinking that Ruby had slipped through his fingers.

But she was right here. Right now.

He ran his palm along her arm. 'I thought about you, Ruby. I thought about you a lot. When you didn't reply to the message I left you I just assumed you'd changed your mind.' He met her gaze again, 'Or that you'd seen the news and didn't want any part of it.'

'Oh, Alex…' She lifted her hand and stroked her fingers through her hair. Her head shook slowly.

'I never got your message, Alex. And once I realised who you were I assumed you didn't want
to know me—plain old Ruby Wetherspoon. You
were a *prince*, for goodness' sake—with a whole
country to look after. I didn't think you'd even remember me.'

He reached up and touched her cheek. 'You have
no idea at all. And you've never been plain old Ruby
to me.'

'The flowers… They were from you—weren't
they?'

He nodded. 'I didn't want to interfere in your life.
But then there came a time when it wasn't appropriate to send them any more.' His chest tightened
as he said the words.

He didn't need to go into detail.

He'd always harboured hopes about Ruby. But
once he'd known he had to make a commitment to
Sophia it had become inappropriate to keep sending flowers to another woman. Alex would never
have done something like that.

'I guess now I'm free to send you flowers again,'
he said quietly.

'I guess you are.'

She gave him a little smile and set down her glass.
The yacht was moving around the coastline, dancing along in the waves—just as they were dancing
around each other.

'Why did you ask me to come, Alex? Why did
you want me here?'

There it was again. That tiny tremble in her voice. He loved the fact that she was fearless. That she was courageous enough to ask the question out loud.

Ruby wasn't bound by a country. Ruby wasn't bound by two whole nations hoping she'd be able to keep them financially stable. Ruby didn't have to bite her tongue to prevent international incidents with foreign diplomats. Ruby had her own life— her own responsibilities. Could he really be honest? Was he willing to expose her to the world he lived in?

It was time to take a risk.

'I didn't just ask you here for Annabelle, Ruby. I need your help with my daughter. That much is clear.' He reached over and took her hand. 'But I asked you here for me too.'

She bit her lip. He could tell she was trying not to interrupt, but she just couldn't help it.

'But what does that *mean*, Alex? I need you to say it out loud.'

She was drawing a line in the sand. And she was right.

He knew she was right.

He met her gaze and touched her cheek. 'I want us to have a chance, Ruby Wetherspoon. I'm not your everyday guy, and what I have isn't your everyday job. I'd like to see where this can take us, but I understand the pressure of being here and being with me. I don't want to expose you to anything before you're ready.'

She shook her head. 'Not enough. Who *am* I, Alex? Am I Ruby Wetherspoon, speech and language therapist for your daughter? Am I Ruby Wetherspoon the hired help who might catch your eye? Or am I Ruby Wetherspoon the girl you might decide to date?'

She stood up and walked across the deck, held on to the railing, looking out over the sea.

'You touch me, Alex. You kiss me. You bring me out on day trips that make my brain spin. What are you doing, Alex? What are *we* doing?'

He stood up to join her, and then slowed his movements as he neared. He didn't want to stand next to her. So he did what was the most natural thing in the world. He stood behind her, his full body against hers, with his arms wrapped around her waist, sheltering her from the sea winds.

He lifted his hand and caught her hair that was blowing in the breeze. 'Ruby, you can be whatever you want to be. But be warned: being around Alex de Castellane isn't easy. If you want to be the woman I date, that's fine. If you want to do that in public or private, that's fine with me too.'

He moved closer to her, whispering in her ear, nuzzling her.

'I lost you once, Ruby. I don't intend to lose you again. But I'll take your lead on this.'

He held his hands out towards the cliffs and the view of Euronia.

'The world out there can be hard. I want to give

this a chance. I want to see where this will take us. I'd love to be able to walk down the street with you without everyone whispering—but that will never happen. I'm public property, Ruby. The world owns me. I don't want it to own you too. At least not until we're both sure about what we want.'

She turned herself towards him, tears glistening in her eyes.

He lowered his hands and wrapped them around her waist. 'What do you say, Ruby? Are you willing to give us a try?'

She wrapped her arms around his neck and stood on her tiptoes, whispering in his ear. 'I think I might need a little extra persuasion.'

'What kind of persuasion?' He liked the thought of where this might go.

'I might have questions. Conditions.'

He was surprised. 'Okay…' he said slowly. 'Like what?'

This time the expression on her face was a little bit cheeky, a little bit naughty. 'If we start dating do I get to look in all the palace rooms that are currently out of bounds to me?'

'*That's* what you want to know?' He couldn't help but smile.

'I also want to check for secret passages and dungeons.'

He nodded solemnly. 'That might be difficult. I'll have to see what I can do.'

'Can I slide down the banister?'

'That might be taking things a bit far.'

She shrugged. 'It'll save the staff from polishing.'

He nodded. 'True.' And then he sighed. 'I wish I'd thought of that explanation twenty years ago. You could have got me out of a whole heap of trouble.'

She stood up and whispered in his ear again. 'How about painting the palace a brighter shade of pink? Doesn't every girl want to live in a pink palace?'

He laughed. 'You don't think it's pink enough already? It might be every girl's dream but guess what? It's not every teenage boy's. I told you—I hated living in a pink palace.'

She shook her head. 'Silly boy. You just don't know what you had.'

He stopped smiling and touched her cheek. 'But I do now.'

She bit her lower lip again. He couldn't help but fixate on it. They weren't entirely alone on this boat. But right now he didn't care. It seemed as if he'd been waiting for this moment for ever.

He bent forward and captured her lips against his. She met him hungrily, pushing herself against him and letting her fingers gently stroke the back of his neck. The sensation shot directly down his spine and into his groin.

He pulled back. There was a whole host of things running through his mind right now. But none was as important as being here with Ruby.

He grabbed her hand and pulled her inside.

'There are seven staff on this boat. They would never disturb us, but things aren't exactly private here. If we're going to see where this takes us we have to agree what you're comfortable with.'

She looked a little unsure. But her face was flushed and her hands were touching his waist— almost as if she didn't want to let go.

He glanced down at them and gave a laugh. 'Careful, Ruby. You've no idea where my *brain's* currently taking us.'

He opened the door and pulled her along a narrow corridor,

'I've made plans for us today. Let's cool off. There are some swimsuits inside this room along here. We'll anchor the boat, do a little swimming, and then have some dinner.' He stopped outside the door of one of the rooms and hesitated. 'It'll give you time to think.'

He was aware that she hadn't said anything—was terrified that he might have frightened her off. Ruby probably hadn't considered the real consequences of being involved with a prince and he'd just laid them all bare to her.

He'd lived with press intrusion all his life. But in his world it was slightly easier for men than women. When the heir to the throne in the United Kingdom had got married his new wife had been constantly under the glare of the spotlight. Even now every outfit she wore, every friend she spoke to, even the appointments in her diary were scrutinised continuously.

Euronia might not be the UK, but it was a hotspot for the rich and famous. The press were always lurking somewhere in the background. He was surprised no one had commented on Ruby's presence before now. She must have slipped under the radar as a member of staff. But that wouldn't last much longer.

Her smile faltered. 'Alex, what if we're making a mistake? What if we're both caught in the memory of ten years ago and what we've imagined and reality is totally different?' She looked up through heavy eyelids. 'We might not even *like* each other.'

His stomach twisted. It was true. It was a fair comment. But it went against his gut. It went against how he truly felt.

He didn't know Ruby that well. Someone, somewhere in the palace would have a report on her—they had one on every staff member. And his security staff would have the report from ten years ago on the woman he'd been with when they'd found him at the café in Paris. Someone would know which schools she'd attended in England, what the occupations of her mum and dad were, if she had any political affiliations.

But he didn't want to find out from a bit of paper. He wanted to find out in real time—with Ruby.

So he did what his gut told him to do. He leaned forward and brushed a kiss against her cheek. 'Then let's find out.'

* * *

She stepped inside and closed the door behind her, instantly feeling the coolness of the air-conditioned room. Her cheek burned from where he'd kissed her.

Kissed her—and left her. Walking down the corridor, leaving her to fixate on his backside and broad shoulders. She felt like someone from a bad movie.

Her stomach was turning over and over. *'Let's find out.'*

She'd waited ten years to find out. Ten years of secret thoughts and wild imagination. Did this mean anything between them was destined to fail?

She picked up her mobile and pressed the quick call button. She'd never needed to talk to someone so badly.

'Polly? Are you free? Can you talk?'

'Ruby? Where on earth have you been? I tried to call you three times yesterday. Are you coming home?'

'No. Not yet. And maybe…'

'Maybe what?' Polly got straight to the point. 'What's happening with you and Prince Perfect?'

Ruby sighed and leaned against the wall. 'He just kissed me, Polly. He kissed me and I didn't want him to stop.'

'Oh, no. Don't start all this dreamy kissing stuff again. Does this guy have stars and rainbows in his lips? One kiss and you go all squishy.'

She smiled. It was true. Trust Polly just to come

out with it. 'I'm worried, Pol. He's told me he wants to give us a chance. He's asked me if I'm willing.'

'Willing to what? Flounce off into the sunset on matching unicorns? What exactly does he need you to be willing *for*?'

'To give us a go. To see where this takes us.' She started to slide down the wall. 'But I can't think straight, Pol. I'm just Ruby. I'm not a princess. I'm not a supermodel. How can I possibly live up to the expectations he has? I don't even know what fork to pick up at dinner.'

'Ruby Wetherspoon, you listen to me. This isn't about his expectations. This is about yours. You don't *need* to be a princess or a supermodel. You're better than both. He is lucky to have met you. He's lucky you agreed to go and help with his daughter. This isn't about you being good enough for him. The question is: is Prince Perfect good enough for *you*?'

Trust Polly. She could always boost her confidence and make her feel better. It was like having her own professional cheerleader and piranha all in one. But whilst she loved what Polly was saying, she just wasn't sure she believed it.

Polly hadn't finished talking. 'And as for the forks—just start on the outside and work your way in. Never fails.'

Ruby was shaking her head. 'I like him, Polly. I really like him. But this is a whole other country. There's so many people watching me. So many people watching *him*.'

'He's a prince, Ruby. What do you want?'

She sighed. 'I want to do normal things. I want to get to know him better. I want the chance to go out and have a glass of wine with him. I want to go to the cinema and fight about who is the best action hero or the best *Star Trek* captain—'

'Picard.' Polly cut her off quickly. 'It's always Picard.'

Ruby heard the squeak of furniture as Polly obviously sat down.

'I hate to break it to you, honey, but going for a glass of wine and heading to the multiplex is probably a no-no. Anyway—doesn't Alex have a whole cinema in the palace?'

'Probably. I don't know. I just can't think straight around him, Pol. He walks in a room and my whole body—it just *tingles*.' She gave a little shake as she said the words.

'Oh, no. No tingling. Definitely no tingling.'

'People here—they're different. The way they treat Alex. The way they treat me when I'm with Alex…'

Her voice drifted off as her train of thought started to take her down the railway line to mild panic.

'His mother spoke four languages. I can't do that. I know nothing about politics. Or history. Or modern studies. I only got a passing grade in geography because I memorised stuff about eroding coastlines.'

'What exactly do you think you're auditioning for here, Rubes? You're a speech and language therapist—an expert in your field. You've published professional papers. You work at one of the finest hospitals in London. Why do you think you're not good enough for him?'

She started shaking her head. 'It's not that I think I'm not good enough. I'm just worried. Alex wants to give us a chance—*I* want to give us a chance—but what about the rest of the world?'

'Hang the rest of the world, Ruby. This is *your* life. Not theirs.' Polly groaned. 'You know I want you back here with me. But *ten years*, Ruby. Ten years you waited for this guy to come back into your life. You can't let what anyone else thinks matter.'

Ruby straightened up. Polly was right. Alex was right. He was just trying to prepare her. Trying to let her understand that things might be difficult.

But Alex de Castellane wanted *her*—Ruby Wetherspoon. It had to mean something.

She walked over to the other side of the cabin. 'Oh, Pol. He's bought me clothes.'

'Again? What is he—a personal shopper or a prince?'

She lifted up a scrap of material from the bed and squinted at it—trying to imagine what it covered. 'Well, they're not clothes, exactly. More like tiny bits of cloth. I think they're supposed to be for swimming.' She started to laugh and shake her head as she moved her phone to snap a picture and send it to Polly. 'What on earth is *that* supposed to cover?'

There were five different styles of swimming costume on the bed, along with a whole host of scraps doing their best impression of itsy-bitsy teeny-weeny bikinis. She picked up the first and checked the label. At least they were her size—but there was no way she was wearing one in front of Alex. Not right now anyway.

There was a screech at the other end of the phone as Polly got the photo. She started howling with laughter. 'Gotta go, honey—the baby's crying. But, please—if you wear that you've got to send me a photo!'

Ruby smiled as the call was disconnected. She always felt better after talking to Polly. But Polly's life had moved on. They were still best friends. But Polly had a husband and a baby. She'd found her happy-ever-after. What about Ruby's?

She picked up a red swimsuit, slightly padded with a ruched front. Perfect. Something that actually covered the parts it should. It only took two minutes to put it on, and she grabbed a sheer black sarong to knot around her waist.

It was time to get out there.

*Let's find out.*

Alex was doing his best impression of a male model in white trunks. She gulped. She was going to have to avert her eyes. Either that or put a sign on her head saying that if she looked at that area it would make her knees go weak.

He was waiting for her out on deck and he led her around to the back of the yacht this time. Again there were some seats, but Alex had also laid down towels on a flat area overhanging the edge. There was no ladder down the side. This flat part seemed to have been designed purely for getting in and out of the sea.

She sat down on a white towel and blushed as she noticed his appreciative gaze. 'What do you normally use this for?'

'Diving. I used to do a lot of diving with friends. Nothing too spectacular. Just for fun. So when I commissioned the yacht I knew I wanted a diving platform attached.'

'You *commissioned* the yacht? You didn't just buy it from a catalogue? Just how rich are you, Alex?'

She was laughing as she said the words and turned to dip her toes in the water. Even though the sun was blistering hot the sea was cold.

'Youch!'

She pulled her feet back in as Alex laughed. 'Here.' He tossed her some sunscreen. 'Put some of this on or you'll burn your nose.'

It was easy to forget how hot the sun was with the sea breezes around them. She smeared some sunscreen on her face, arms and legs, then stood behind him, poised to put some cream on his back.

But he grabbed her arm and pulled her into his

lap. 'I've already got some. You, however, need some on *your* back. Give me that.'

He squirted some cream on his hands and started to rub it over her back. She was almost scared to move. Her position was precarious. They were right at the edge of the moored boat and she was balancing on his knees. Right now there were only two very thin pieces of fabric separating them. Her right arm was pressing against his bare chest, the dark curling hairs tickling her skin.

His hand movements slowed, going from initially brisk and efficient to sensual, circling her back, slipping under the straps on her shoulders and smearing cream across every part of her skin. She breathed in sharply and his hand circled lower, fingertips sweeping below her swimsuit.

His voice was husky, his accent thicker. 'You didn't like the bikinis?'

'I didn't like *me* in the bikinis.'

'Why ever not?' His fingers slowed and stopped, staying just underneath the back of her costume. 'You're a beautiful woman, Ruby.'

She felt her cheeks flush, instantly embarrassed by his words—which was ironic, really, since she was sitting half clothed in his lap. Could anyone see them, sitting here on the back of his yacht? In front of her all she could see was the Mediterranean Sea. There wasn't even another boat in sight.

His hand moved gently around her waist, touching the fabric of her costume and resting next to the knot of her sarong. 'This is definitely your colour. You suit red, Ruby. It seems as though your mother named you well.'

'My mother named me after the ruby slippers in *The Wizard of Oz*. But I'll tell her you appreciate her choice,' she teased.

This was too much. She was sitting here, feeling the rise and fall of his chest next to her arm, the warmth between his skin and hers. Their faces were inches apart. Not touching him properly was torture.

She moved that little inch, putting her hand at the back of his head and tugging him closer until their lips touched. His fingers started tugging at the knot on her sarong. It fell apart easily.

The kiss quickly intensified. She could easily tell the effect their close contact was having on his body—just as it was having an effect on hers. Kissing him was too easy.

They weren't in Paris any more. It wasn't New Year's Eve. But she could almost hear the fireworks going off in her head.

The sun wasn't heating her skin any more—Alex was. Every nibble, every tiny touch of his tongue electrified her. She let out a little moan as their kiss deepened, his hands running up and down the bare skin on her back.

'Ruby…' he muttered.

'What?' She didn't want him to stop. She didn't want this moment to end.

'We're out in the open. I know it doesn't feel like it, but...' His voice tailed off.

She was still kissing him, never wanting it to end.

A few minutes ago the sea had seemed deserted. But other boats had passed them on their journey around the coastline. And the crew might not come down here, but if she didn't stop this now...she might live to regret it.

She broke the kiss. 'Alex?'

'What?' He looked up, those gorgeous blue eyes connecting with hers.

She smiled. 'You're right. It's time to cool off.'

Her arms were still wrapped around him and she just leaned backwards, pulling them both into the cold blue sea.

The plunge was a little further than she'd expected, and the shock of the cold water on her skin pushed the air from her lungs as it closed around her. It only took a few seconds to push to the surface and break out into the warm sun. She was laughing and coughing and spluttering all at once.

She slicked her wet hair back from her face as Alex surfaced next to her, shaking his head and showering her with droplets of water.

'This is getting to be a habit,' he said as he swam next to her and put his hands around her waist underwater.

The cold water was doing nothing to dampen their desire and she wound her hands around his neck again as they trod water.

'It is, isn't it? Maybe you and I shouldn't be around water.' She laughed.

'What should we be around?' he asked as the waves buoyed them up.

'I don't know. Pink palaces, Eiffel Towers, fireworks and yellow dresses.' She could see the twinkle in his eye as she said those last words.

'Come on,' he gestured towards her. 'Let's swim around the boat. It might be best if we have some water between us.'

Her hand touched his arm as they separated in the water.

They laughed and swam around the boat, occasionally stopping next to each other as Alex told her a little more about his country.

'The caves down there were traditionally used by pirates.'

There were two dark caves carved into the bottom of the cliffs on the rocky shoreline. Her body had grown accustomed to the temperature of the water but she still gave a shudder.

'No way. Fairytales. Made-up stories.'

He lifted his hand out of the water. 'You forget— this is a land with a pink palace. You think we didn't have pirates?'

'When you put it like that it doesn't seem quite so crazy.'

'I'll show you some of the things in the castle vaults. I think my ancestors might have been in league with the pirates. Either that or they just kept everything once they'd captured the pirates.'

'Are you allowed to do that?'

He shrugged his shoulders as they continued to swim around the boat. 'We have some old doubloons, some jewellery and some weapons. The assumption is that they are Spanish, but the Spaniards didn't want them back when they were offered a few hundred years ago. There isn't enough to be of any real value—we've kept them safe because of the historical importance.'

She kept swimming. 'I'm going to add that to my list of conditions from earlier—a visit to the pirate caves.' She winked, 'I might even ask you to dress up.'

As they rounded the hull of the yacht another boat came into view. It was not quite as big as Alex's, but equally sleek in white and silver.

Alex sighed. 'Let's get back on board.'

'Do you know who owns that boat?'

He stroked out towards the diving platform. 'It's Randall Merr and his wife. They can be unbearable. I'll tell the crew to head back to port.'

Randall Merr. A billionaire with houses all over the world—including in Euronia.

Part of her stomach twisted. Maybe Alex didn't want to introduce her to his friends? Maybe he was embarrassed by her?

She put her head in the water and struck out towards the platform. Alex reached it first and turned round to help her out of the water, offering her a towel and her sarong.

The electricity between them seemed to have dissipated. All of a sudden she felt very exposed—and it wasn't because she was wearing only swimwear. The magic bubble that she'd felt earlier around her and Alex had vanished in the blink of an eye.

'Ruby, what's wrong?'

He was picking up the other towels and the sunscreen from around them.

She started up the steps. 'Nothing's wrong. I'm going to put some clothes on.' She hated that tiny waver in her voice.

He caught her arm. 'Ruby, tell me what's wrong. Are you angry with me?'

The words that were spinning around in her brain tumbled out of her mouth unchecked. Nothing she would ever really want him to hear.

'Why would I be angry with you, Alex? You tell me it's up to *me* to decide how this goes—then as soon as we see someone you know you try and bundle me away. As if I'm some kind of employee you can't be seen with. Which, when you think about it, I really am—aren't I?'

His brow crumpled and confusion swept over his face. He shook his head and tightened his grip on her arm, pulling her hard against him. She was above him, on the first step of the stairs. Their faces were perfectly level.

'You think I want to hide you? After everything I've said?'

His nose was almost touching hers and his eyes were blazing. She'd angered him.

But instead of being intimidated she just felt another fire spark within her. 'Well, that's what it looks like.'

His lips connected with hers. His hands jerked her hipbones against his. This was no delicate kiss. This was no teasing, no playing with her. This was pure and utter passion.

His hands moved from her hips and his fingers tangled in her hair, tugging her head one way then another. His teeth clashed with hers and his tongue drove its way into her mouth. She could hardly breathe. He was devouring her.

He finally released her just as the white boat passed directly behind the yacht. It was so close the yacht bobbed wildly in its wake.

'There,' he growled, without even turning around. 'Randall Merr and his wife got a prime-time view. If you didn't want anyone to know about us it's too late. That woman practically has a satellite connection to the world's press.'

She gulped. Was that really what she wanted?

Truth was, she hadn't answered Alex because she was unsure.

She wasn't unsure about him. Not for a second. But she was definitely unsure about his world.

How could she possibly ever fit in to his lifestyle?

She was already sure that some of the staff didn't like her and suspected something might be in the air between them.

She wanted the Alex she'd met ten years ago in Paris. The gorgeous, slightly mysterious man with a bit of an accent.

But that wasn't Alex at all. *This* was Alex. The acting ruler of one country and potentially the temporary head of another. The father of a young daughter. The son of a sick man. A businessman with the financial responsibility for all the inhabitants of his country.

Her Alex had only really ever existed in her head.

And whilst the living, breathing Alex in front of her was sexier than she could ever have dreamed of, she was still wondering if this was all a figment of her imagination.

After ten years he'd come looking for her.

After ten years he'd told her he'd let her decide the pace.

She was finding it hard to believe it. These were the kind of dreams she'd had ten years ago and never told anyone about.

Alex de Castellane had spent his life surrounded by supermodels and movie stars. They all flocked to his country—a tax haven. They all wanted to be seen with him, to be photographed with him.

And Alex, Prince Regent, was charming. He knew how to show interest and talk to people as if they were the only ones in the room. There was something enigmatic about him. And for most people it would be easy to get lost in his world.

But Ruby was different. Ruby wasn't looking for a fairytale.

Maybe the Alex she'd always imagined was just a figment of her imagination. Maybe he'd never really existed.

The man she'd spent a few hours with that night had been excited about life. Had had plans for the future. He'd offered to show her around Paris and she had gladly accepted.

Accepted the chance to spend a few more hours in his company. Accepted the chance to be the focus of his attention for a few more hours.

Would she have accepted any of it if she'd known his real identity?

Most of the world would have screamed *yes*. Most of the world would have claimed it was every girl's dream to be a princess. But most of the world wasn't Ruby Wetherspoon.

Her hand was still on his arm. Droplets of sea water were running down his skin, running from his hair down his chest. Physically, she wanted Alex. Emotionally, she wanted Alex. Mentally, she wanted Alex. But all wrapped up together?

It was terrifying. And she couldn't put it into words. She didn't know how to explain the feeling of wanting to reach out and grab him, yet feeling totally overwhelmed.

Right now she wanted to be back in her room

at the palace. The room next to Annabelle's. She wanted to be curled up with Annabelle, watching a movie and observing her. In an environment of peace and calm. In a place where she felt safe.

A place where she didn't feel so exposed.

'Get changed. Ruby. Put some clothes on. I'll meet you back on deck and we'll have some food, then go back to the palace.'

The Alex of earlier was lost. The man who'd looked at her almost adoringly and whispered in her ear had vanished from her grasp.

The warm sea breeze had turned distinctly chilly. It swept around her, making every little hair on her arms stand to attention. She wrapped the towel around her shoulders.

Her feet slipped and squelched along the wooden-floored corridor until she finally reached the room with her clothes and she sagged down, wet and cold, onto the bed.

All of a sudden the designer bathing suits didn't seem quite so attractive any more.

She lay down on the bed—just for a second—and closed her eyes.

# CHAPTER EIGHT

ALEX WAS HAVING trouble keeping his emotions in check.

Today, all he'd been able to think about was Ruby. He hadn't worried about share prices. About price indexes. About gas, electricity and oil prices.

Today he'd just thought about the beautiful, bright-eyed woman in front of him. For a time it had seemed perfect.

Their familiarity and warmth had developed over the last few weeks and he'd finally managed to put into words the things that had been circulating in his brain.

Then—*bam!* It felt as if everything was ruined.

He was pacing up and down the deck. The crew all seemed to have vanished into the mists—as if they knew he was brooding. Cold diet colas had appeared magically in a silver cooler. His steward had obviously realised that this wasn't the time for more champagne.

He couldn't even face eating right now. So much was circulating in his head that his stomach was churning over and over.

How had he managed to mess this up? He'd planned it in his head. *Give her time to think about this. Don't rush her.* He was sure he'd seen a flicker of doubt in her eyes and that had almost killed him. He was treading so carefully around her.

Then the Merrs and their darn boat. Mrs Merr had probably buzzed them deliberately. Anything to see what the Prince Regent was up to.

He'd thought he was giving Ruby time. He'd thought he was giving her space. Wasn't that what she wanted?

But a few moments ago she'd seemed angry—annoyed that he'd tried to hide her from prying eyes. He'd only been trying to protect her. But her words had practically sent a flare up.

He wanted to be seen with Ruby. He wanted to tell the world that he was willing to take a chance on where this might go.

But he was also terrified that harsh treatment by the world's press would send her running for the hills.

How on earth was he supposed to know what was right and what was wrong?

Would he ever be able to fathom the way Ruby's brain worked?

Right now it seemed unlikely.

He glanced at his watch. She hadn't appeared. He went into his cabin, pulled out his laptop and sat at the table.

Time. That was what he needed to give her.

In the meantime, he still had work to do.

* * *

Ruby hovered at the glass doors. He was concentrating fiercely on the laptop screen in front of him.

She'd sat down on the bed for just a minute and ended up sleeping for an hour. When she'd woken she'd been embarrassed. But it had been too late for that, so she'd showered and changed before coming out.

She'd half expected to find the boat moored back in the harbour, and was pleasantly surprised to find they were still out at sea.

Here, there was nowhere to run and hide. Here, she would need to talk to Alex.

She'd changed into a turquoise-blue maxi-dress and flat jewelled sandals and pulled her hair up into a ponytail. She wasn't trying to seduce Alex. She wasn't trying to entice him away from anything else.

She was here to have one of the hardest conversations of her life.

This had all crept up on her. She'd known it was always there—hovering in the background. But things had become crystal-clear to her.

It was so easy to think that this was about her. About whether she could stand the press attention or not. But it wasn't really. It was about him. She just had to be brave enough to say the words.

Her stomach growled loudly and he turned sharply in his chair.

'Ruby.'

It was more like a grunt than a greeting—not a good start. But it gave her the kick she needed. She took the few steps across the cabin and pulled out the chair opposite him.

'Sorry. I sat down for five minutes and fell asleep.'

'You obviously don't find my company riveting enough.'

It was a barb. And she could take it or she could react.

She leaned over and snapped the laptop shut on his fingers. 'Got your attention now?'

He snatched his fingers back and glared at her. 'I was working.'

'You're always working.'

It was as if all the barriers around them had come crashing down. Right now she wasn't afraid to say anything—and from the looks of it neither was he.

'Make up your mind what you want, Ruby.'

'I can't. There's too many variables.'

No nice words. No beating about the bush. Two people with everything at stake.

'Well, let's start with the things that can't change. The non-variables.'

She leaned over and grabbed a can from the silver bucket, popping the tab and taking a sip. This could take a while.

'Is this like a quiz show, Alex? Do I win something if I get the questions right?'

Their eyes locked. They both knew exactly

what was at stake here. They both knew what the prize was.

He sucked in a deep breath and held his hand out for the can of cola. It was the first sign that this really was going to be a discussion.

His voice was low. 'I'm always going to be the King of Euronia. I'm always going to be father to Annabelle.'

She nodded. 'I've never questioned those things.'

He held her gaze. 'But I've never really told you that those are things that I *wanted*. Not just things that were forced upon me or inherited by birth. When I was young I thought being King would be a whole lot of pressure on my shoulders—with no say in it for me. As I've grown older I've accepted that not only is this my destiny, it's something I actually want.'

She ran her tongue along her lips. Deep down she'd always known this. Even though Alex hadn't told her who he was when they'd met. This wasn't just his inherited future. This was a future he was willing to embrace.

It was a first step. It was the first time he'd actually admitted to her what he wanted in life.

He leaned back in his chair a little. 'I went to the US to study and learn business. It was my idea, not my father's, but he fully supported it. The world is changing constantly—it's getting smaller—and Euronia needed to move into the twenty-first century.'

'And now?'

'Now I need to use everything that I've learned to help my country prosper.'

'So where does that leave us?'

So many things were sparking in her brain. Did Alex suspect what she was about to say to him?

'How do you feel about me, Ruby?'

The question blind-sided her. She knew they were having a frank discussion, but she hadn't expected him just to ask her outright.

'I…' Her voice tailed off as her brain tried frantically to find the right words.

He shook his head.

She hadn't even answered yet and she'd disappointed him. But how could she tell him how she really felt when they still hadn't dealt with the heart of the problem? She had to say the words.

'What if Sophia had lived?'

'What?' He looked confused. Blind-siding worked both ways.

'What if her cancer had been cured and she'd lived—what then?'

He shook his head. 'That would never have happened. Sophia's cancer was already terminal. Nothing was going to change that.'

'But what if it had? Would you still have married her? Still have had Annabelle? Would you have come looking for me at all?'

Her voice started to shake a little and she took a deep breath. She needed to be calm. She needed to be rational and not blinded by her emotions.

'I need you to be honest with me, Alex. I need you to be honest with yourself.' This was hurting more than she could ever have imagined. 'If Sophia was alive today, where would she feature in your life?'

'Don't paint her as the villain in this piece. You're angry with me because I married another woman. Just say it.' He blurted it out straight away.

'You're right. I *was* angry. More than that, I was bitterly disappointed—even though I'd no right to be. But I don't understand. If you'd really wanted to find me you could have. In fact, you did. You sent me those flowers. Why didn't you just come and see me? Why didn't you ever jump in your million-pound jet and come and find me?'

She was sounding desperate and she hated herself for being like that. But if it was going to be all out there—then so be it.

'You didn't answer my message, Ruby. I left you a message—I got no reply. What was I supposed to do? Search for a woman who didn't want me to find her? Embarrass myself and put you in vulnerable position?'

She bit her lip. It was a reasonable reply. But it didn't make her like it any better.

He kept going.

'I thought my father was about to die. The things I'd been working towards were being thrust on me from a great height. I didn't have time to think about it any more—I had to just do it. No wonder my father had agreed for me to study business. The country's finances were in a mess. We were teetering on the brink of disaster. For the best part of three years I juggled finances, moved money, invested money, watched stock markets and persuaded people to come to Euronia—persuaded people to invest in Euronia. Most nights I got around four hours' sleep. I was a mess, Ruby. I didn't have time to sleep, let alone think. How would you have felt if you'd been around a man who was too busy to spend time with you? Too busy to talk? Too busy to sleep? What kind of a relationship would that have been?'

'But you found time for Sophia.'

She said it so quietly the words were barely a whisper above the hum of the yacht's engines.

Alex's eyes widened and his response was immediate. 'Sophia appeared just as things were starting to look up. She was desperate, Ruby. She was dying and she was my friend. Sophia's illness brought me back to reality. What's the point of taking care of a country if you can't take care of those around you?'

She could hear the emotion in his voice. It was starting to break. This was it. This was the whole crux of the matter. This was the enormous big grey elephant in the room and it was time to smash it to smithereens.

'So what happened with Annabelle, then?'

The words echoed around them. She hadn't really meant to say them out loud. They'd come into her brain and out of her mouth almost instantly. It was cruel. It was uncalled for.

It was unintentional.

He sat back sharply—almost as if she'd thrust a knife into his chest.

'You think it's my fault, don't you?'

She looked him straight in the eye. Everyone had danced around Alex. Everyone had chosen their words carefully. But this was it. This was the only way to give them a fighting chance.

'I think that when Sophia died Annabelle didn't just lose her mother, she lost her father too.'

She took a deep breath and continued.

'You keep claiming Sophia was only your friend. And you can tell me that as often as you like. But your little girl is the spitting image of her mother. Do you think I've not noticed that there's no photograph of her mother in her room? Do you think I don't see that little fleeting gaze of something when you look at her? Don't ask me what it is, Alex, but it's there. I've seen it. Children pick up on these things. And I think Annabelle has picked up on it. You don't want to be around her. She reminds you too much of what you've lost.'

She could almost see the shock registering on his face, but she couldn't stop.

She pointed her finger at him. 'I know you've been busy, but I don't think you've been as busy as you claim to be. When I laid it out for you that you *had* to spend time with her you managed to do it.'

She was hurting him. She could tell. And she really didn't want to. But it had to be said. She had to try and move them both forward.

'She's improving, Alex. She is. I know that when she's around you, and around me, she exists in her own little bubble. But it's our job to expand your daughter's world in a way that makes her feel safe.'

'This isn't about Annabelle. Today isn't about Annabelle. This is supposed to be about you and me.'

He looked stunned. Stunned that someone had challenged him on his feelings about Sophia. Stunned that someone was suggesting the reason his daughter might not be speaking was his fault.

It was only natural for him to try and deflect the conversation.

'But it can't be, Alex. It can't be until you deal with this first.' She kept her voice steady. 'Tomorrow I'm going to find the nicest photo I can of Sophia and put it in a frame next to Annabelle's bed. She needs to be able to look at her mother every day. She needs to know that there was someone in this world who loved and adored her.'

'You mean I don't?'

He was furious. His eyes were blazing. But no matter how much it made her stomach ache this was exactly what she had to do.

'Don't you get it, Alex? There can't be an "us". There can't be the start of anything between us until you face up to your past. Annabelle wasn't created in a dish. She wasn't a test tube baby. You slept with your wife. You created a child together. Part of you loved her.'

She waved her hand.

'Stop trying to tell me otherwise. I've accepted it, Alex, and so must you. If you want us to be seen together—if you want to kiss me like that again—then it has to be on the condition that you've grieved for your wife. It has to be on the condition that you can look at your daughter and love her the way you should.'

Tears started to roll down her cheeks.

'This isn't about me trying to decide if I want to be seen in public with you or not. I can't even answer that yet—because we're not there yet. It's easy for you to put all the responsibility for this relationship on my shoulders. Because then you don't need to think about Sophia or Annabelle at all.'

The tears wouldn't stop. Her heart was breaking.

Alex's face had crumpled. She didn't have a single doubt that she loved this man sitting across from her. This proud, passionate, potential king.

It would be so easy to get swept along with the wonder of the pink palace, Euronia, and a prince who'd come looking for her after ten years.

She wanted him for herself. She really did.

She almost wished she could take back everything she'd just said and walk through that door again and wrap her arms around his neck and kiss him.

But this would always have been there.

This would eventually have festered between them.

She wanted to be free to love Alex. And she wanted him to be free to love her. Things just didn't feel like that right now.

'This is killing me, Alex,' she whispered.

He stood up sharply, his chair screeching along the floor. He ran his fingers through his hair. 'I need to think. I need to think about all this.'

His eyes were vacant. As if he couldn't look at her, couldn't focus.

The tables had turned completely.

He'd been telling *her* to take her time.

But the reality was after ten years it was Alex who needed to take his time.

She stood up and walked back towards the glass doors.

This time it was her turn to say the words. 'Take all the time you need.'

# CHAPTER NINE

For two days he avoided Ruby.

There was too much to think about—too much to absorb.

Any time he was around Ruby he was drawn to her and wanted to touch her.

But horrible little parts of what she'd said were keeping him awake at night.

The photograph part was easy. He knew exactly which picture to frame for Annabelle. It was embarrassing to think he hadn't even considered it before.

He—and the advisors around him—had just assumed that Annabelle wouldn't remember anything about her mother.

He hadn't deliberately kept her pictures away from Annabelle—he just hadn't thought to talk to Annabelle about her mother.

She was playing in her room now. One blonde doll seemed to be driving a racing car around the furniture and over most of the other toys. She was making noises again—a *brrrrmm* for the racing car and a gasp as the doll plummeted over the bedcovers.

His heart twisted in his chest. If Sophia had lived would their little girl have been like this? It was a horrible thing to consider. It meant facing up to facts—facing up to a responsibility that he'd thought he had fulfilled.

Ruby thought differently.

He couldn't hesitate any longer. He walked into the room, keeping his voice bright. 'Hi, Annabelle. I've brought a picture for you.'

He put the silver frame on Annabelle's bedside table.

There was an audible gasp. It almost ripped him in two.

The picture was almost exactly at Annabelle's head height. She tilted her head to one side, her eyes wide.

He could have picked from a million pictures of Sophia. Once Annabelle was old enough to use the internet she would find another million pictures of her mother online.

But this was his favourite. This had always been his favourite. It was the picture he still had of Sophia in his mind—not the frail, emaciated pale woman she'd become.

This picture had Sophia on a swing, her blonde hair streaming behind her, her face wide with laughter and her pink dress billowing around her. She was around eighteen in this picture and it captured her perfectly. It captured the fun-loving human being she'd been before illness had struck her down.

He had other pictures. Pictures of her holding Annabelle not long after the birth and in the following months. There were lots of those.

But all of those pictures were touched with inherent sadness. The inevitability of a life lost. He'd put some into a little album for Annabelle. Those were for another day.

She reached out and touched the photo, obviously captivated by the joy in the picture. That was the word it conjured in his brain. *Joy.*

He knelt beside her. 'That's your mama, Annabelle. She was a very beautiful woman and you look just like her. I thought it was time for you to have a photograph of your own.'

Her little brow furrowed for a moment. He could almost see her brain trying to assimilate the information. Her lips moved, making the M movement—but no sound came out.

He rested her hand at her back. 'Look—your dress is the same colour as hers.'

He could see the recognition on his little girl's face. His whole body ached. Why hadn't he done this sooner?

A wave of shame washed over him. He should have known to do this. He should have known that his daughter needed this. But Alex had no experience around children. He had no relatives with youngsters, and as an only child he didn't have much experience to draw on.

He'd had friends—peers—during his life. Sophia had been among them, as had his schoolmates and university friends. But he hadn't been exposed to a life of looking after other people's children.

His sole experience of children before the birth of Annabelle had been on royal tours, where he was expected to talk to kids and hold babies. That was all fine, but it only lasted minutes. It didn't give him a taste of real life.

He looked down at the little girl in front of him. She'd gone back to her dolls and was racing them around the room again. Just like any three-year-old should.

His eyes glanced between his daughter and the photo. The wave of grief was overwhelming. Ruby was right. Sophia *hadn't* just been his friend.

Would he have married her if she hadn't been sick? Probably not. Their relationship hadn't been destined to go that way. Sophia had had wanderlust. She would likely have travelled and married someone from a distant country.

But the genetics of life had changed all that.

He took a deep breath. He hadn't felt the surge of emotion around Sophia that he felt around Ruby. There hadn't been that instant connection. More like a slow-growing respect. But other than Ruby she was the only woman on this planet he'd actually felt anything for.

In his head it had all been about duty and loyalty. He hadn't wanted to let his heart get involved. But if he wanted to move on with Ruby he had to acknowledge that she'd been more than just a friend.

He held his hand out to Annabelle. 'Annabelle,

honey. Come with Daddy. We're going to go and put some flowers on your mama's grave.'

Another tiny step. Another massive milestone.

When was the last time he'd visited Sophia's grave?

He knew for sure he'd never taken his daughter there.

That was all about to change.


The changes were subtle at first.

The first thing she noticed was the picture in the silver frame next to Annabelle's bed. It made her heart squeeze in her chest. One, because he'd done it himself, and two, because Annabelle's mother had indeed been beautiful.

She wasn't jealous. She couldn't bring herself to be jealous of a dead woman. Those initial little pangs of frustration had disappeared. On dark nights—for some horrible moments—she'd wanted this woman never to have existed. Irrational and unreasonable thoughts had filled her head momentarily: Sophia had stolen those ten years she could have had with Alex.

All nonsense.

Life was life.

There was a gorgeous little girl running about around her legs and that was what she should focus on.

Her brain could be logical. It could tell her that

she was there to do a job. It could tell her that she was the best person possible for Annabelle.

And there were discernible changes in Annabelle. Small ones—as if the little girl's walls were being finally worn down.

She wasn't quite so reserved. Her play and interaction at the nursery had changed. Humming was rapidly becoming normal now. Little noises, little sounds would be made with excitement—or sometimes fright if they were watching *Finding Nemo* again.

A small flick-through book of photographs of Annabelle and her mother had appeared. The picture on the front was amazing. One half in black and white, one half in colour. Annabelle and her mother, both sitting on the fountain, at around the same age. Two captured moments in time.

Anyone who didn't know Annabelle would think it was the same little girl.

Ruby could already predict that in her teenage years Annabelle would blow up that picture for her bedroom wall.

The first time she'd flicked through the book with Annabelle talking her through the pictures had been hard. A weight had pressed down on her chest and it had been all she could do to stop the tears rolling down her cheeks. But it became easier, and soon part of their routine every day involved five minutes of flicking through the photos.

It had also become part of Alex's bedtime routine

with Annabelle. The staff had finally got the message and stopped queuing outside the door at night. Alex was adamant that this time was Annabelle's.

And it had done them both good. Alex was more relaxed around his child. He knew what her favourite foods were. He knew who her best friends were at nursery. He could sing along to all the songs in *Finding Nemo*. And gradually the sad tone in his voice was replaced as he told stories of happy memories while they flicked through the photo album.

Ruby stayed in the background although she was working tirelessly with Annabelle. There were no more romantic interludes with Alex, no matter how much she hoped for them. No other heated moments when the air was so thick a wrecking ball couldn't pound its way through.

He still watched her. Sometimes when she lifted her head she would meet his bright blue gaze. The sparks were still there. They were both just treading more warily.

If they brushed hands as they played with Annabelle, or if he moved closer for any reason, the buzz thrummed through her body. Every part of her still wanted to be with him. But she was more confident around him.

She didn't feel the need to look like a supermodel. She didn't feel outclassed by visiting royalty. Alex wanted her. She knew it. He knew it.

Getting there was a slow process. But she could live with that.

Every day she learned something new about Euronia. About its history—the subterfuge, the pirates and the Kings. The history was chequered with colourful characters. Alex's father was probably the quietest ruler of them all.

He was still in Switzerland. Once Alex had flown there, when his father had suffered another bout of pneumonia and had to be ventilated. She'd offered to go but he'd asked her to stay with Annabelle. They both knew the little girl needed stability and she'd been happy to oblige.

The long summer came to a close around the end of September, when Ruby finally had to pull her cardigans out of her cupboard to cover her arms.

And before the leaves on the trees started to change colour Alex started to appear around her again.

At first it was simple. Coffee. Cake. Days sitting in the late summer sunshine in the café in the square. Their visits became so frequent that the café owner stopped asking her what she wanted. After she fawned over a new apricot sponge the café owner started to bake it for her every other day.

Then there was the lunches, and their time spent together that included Annabelle. Sometimes it was in the palace grounds. Sometimes it was in and around Euronia. Once he even took them to Monaco for the day.

This time it felt as if she was the one with the barriers in place and it was Alex who was chipping away at her walls. But it felt right. The momentum was building at a pace that felt comfortable for both of them, for Annabelle, and for the people around them.

Clothes kept mysteriously appearing in her wardrobe—all of them beautiful, all of them fitting perfectly. The palace staff had stopped being prickly around her. Her devotion to Annabelle was clear, but Alex's respect for her was even clearer. Even Rufus had started to come round, and had given her a key to the palace library so she could work undisturbed.

'Ruby?'

Her head shot up. It was late at night and she was sitting on one of the ancient chaise longues, with her feet tucked up underneath her, reading on her electronic tablet.

There were no fancy clothes tonight. Tonight she was wearing a sloppy white top, grey jogging trousers, and her hair was tied in a knot on top of her head.

'Is something wrong with Annabelle?'

It was the first thought that came into her head.

Alex crossed into the room, holding up his hand as he walked. 'No. She's fine. I was looking for you. I should have known I'd find you in here.'

There was a warmth in his eyes as he said the words, a flicker of a memory, and she remembered he'd told her this had been his mother's favourite room.

He pointed at the tablet. 'Isn't it sacrilege to read that in here?'

She shrugged. 'I couldn't work the ancient light switches. Every time I pressed one it seemed to light up the wrong part of the library. Plus, I like being in the dark.'

She pointed to the gardens outside, where some light from the fountain and its walls was spilling up to meet them.

'There's something nice about looking out over the world.'

She turned to face him.

'What have you got?'

He was holding something wrapped in brown paper in his hand, along with two large cups. The smell of something wonderful was winding its way through the air towards her.

'Midnight snacks.' He grinned as he sat down next to her. 'I was starving and went for a rummage around the kitchen to see what I could find.'

She lifted her eyebrows. 'I'm surprised Rufus's inbuilt internal alarm didn't go off at you stepping into the palace kitchens unattended.'

He shrugged. 'I was too. Here,' he handed one of the cups to her and she lifted it to her nose, inhaling.

'Soup?' She glanced at her watch. 'At one in the morning?'

He smiled. That goofy smile he sometimes gave when it was just the two of them. 'I'm hungry. Leena's soup is the best there is.' He held up the brown paper package. 'I even managed to find some freshly baked rolls.'

She opened it up and looked in. Fresh crusty bread in the middle of the night did have a certain appeal.

'Come on,' he said. 'It's no fun eating on your own.'

There was a twinkle in his eye. It was the most relaxed she'd seen him for a while. Spending time with his daughter was doing him the world of good. This wasn't the uptight guy who'd visited her months ago in her hospital department. This wasn't the guy who'd looked as if a permanent grey cloud was resting on his shoulders.

She moved over to the table and he joined her, breaking open his bread roll and dipping it into the soup.

'I've got something else to show you.'

He pushed a file across the table towards her. It was pale beige and looked official.

She flipped it open and gasped. A picture of her and Alex from ten years ago in Paris.

He shrugged. 'It always bothered me that you never got my message. I trust my Head of Security. If he said he sent it I know he did. I had to work out what went wrong.'

'After all this time?'

It had always bothered her too. She'd assumed an absent-minded clerk just hadn't bothered passing the message on.

She looked at the file again. Read the notes. All of them were about her. It was more than a little unnerving. Then she let out a gasp. 'Oh, no!'

His hands closed over hers. 'What is it?'

She smiled at him. 'Hotel du Chat. That's not where I was staying. It says in the notes that your Head of Security left a message at Reception there.'

Alex's brow furrowed. 'He did. But that's what you told me.'

She squeezed his hand. 'Hotel du Champ, Alex. Not Hotel du Chat.' She shook her head. 'After all these years I don't know if that makes me feel better or worse.'

Alex put his head in his hands. 'I was so sure. So sure you said Hotel du Chat.'

'It was noisy, Alex. It was New Year's. You'd just had an urgent message about your father.' She took a deep breath. 'Mistakes happen.'

His finger reached up and touched her cheek. 'I hate mistakes,' he whispered.

'So do I.'

They sat in silence for a few seconds. Both of them letting the revelation wash over them. For Ruby, it felt like a relief. It didn't matter that Alex had assured her he'd tried to contact her. There had always been a tiny sliver of doubt.

But he had. And, strangely, it made her feel good. Maybe life would have been different. Who could possibly know? What she did know was that they couldn't change the past.

'What did the message say?' She couldn't help but ask. It had always played on her mind.

He gave a little nod and held her gaze. 'It was simple.' He shrugged. 'We'd just met and barely had a chance to get to know each other. It said that I was sorry I couldn't meet you, that I really wanted to see you again but had been called away to a family emergency—something I really wanted to explain to you. I left my number and asked you to call as soon as you got my note.'

She gave a sad kind of smile. 'And that—as they say—was that.'

They sat in silence again for a few seconds, thinking of what-might-have-been.

There was no point second-guessing now. Time had passed. They'd found each other again. What happened next was up to them.

Alex pointed back to her soup. 'Better eat that before it gets cold.'

She nodded and picked up her spoon. 'This makes me feel as if I'm in one of those boarding schools that Enid Blyton wrote about and we're having a midnight feast.'

His brow wrinkled. 'She was a kids' author, wasn't she? I must have missed those books.' He gave her a wink. 'Boarding school wasn't so bad.'

'You went to boarding school?' She was fascinated.

'Not until I was twelve. I went to primary school

here in Euronia. The same one that I'm planning on sending Annabelle to.'

Her bread was poised over the cup. 'Do you plan on sending her to boarding school when she's older?'

It was almost as if a little breeze had chilled her skin. It was all right joking about these things, but the thought of Annabelle going to boarding school in a few years made her blood run cold.

'I don't know that much about girls' boarding schools. Maybe... I'd need to see how she was doing first.'

It was a touch of relief, but not enough. She had no business saying anything. But she didn't care.

'I don't think you should.' The words were out before she'd thought about them.

'You don't?'

He seemed surprised. But the atmosphere between them was still relaxed. She felt able to continue.

'I just wonder if that will be the right environment for Annabelle.' She leaned across the table and touched his arm. 'I've something to tell you about today.'

'What is it?'

She gave him a smile. 'Today, when I was at the nursery watching Annabelle, I'm almost sure she spoke to another child.'

'What?'

She nodded. 'She was with a little boy. They were

playing together. I was at the other side of the nursery but I saw her look up and her lips moved. The
little boy's head snapped up, so she must have said
something. But at that point she resorted to signing
again. It was almost as if his reaction reminded her
that she didn't talk.'

Alex looked as if he could hardly believe her. His
face was a mixture of surprise and relief. 'But you
didn't actually hear her?'

'No. I was too far away—and, believe me, it's
bedlam in the nursery. The noise levels are incredible.'

'So, this is good. Isn't it?'

'I hope so. It's one of the concepts of selective
mutism that in some situations children will talk
and in others they won't.'

'What do you think?'

'I think that I can see changes all the time, Alex.
They're slow, but steady. In my head, Annabelle is
a little flower with all its petals tightly closed. It's
only now that she's starting to bloom. We need to
nurture her. We need to keep letting her develop at
her own pace, her own speed.'

He nodded. 'I think so too. I didn't want to say
anything, but when we were flicking through the
pictures the other day it was almost as if the "mmm"
sound was hovering around her lips. It wasn't quite
there, it wasn't quite formed, but I could almost hear
it in the air around us.'

'You think she was going to say Mum?'

He gave a rueful smile. His fingers moved. She was still touching his hand and this time he interlinked his fingers with hers.

'You think I'm just being silly? Is it just a father's wishful thinking?'

She shook her head. He was so sincere.

'I think you're being the same as any parent, Alex. You're putting the welfare of your child first.'

'And so are you.'

He said the words so quietly they took a few seconds to sink into her brain.

His bright blue eyes were fixed on her. The implication was clear. Alex was acknowledging something that she hadn't yet acknowledged herself.

Her other hand was still poised over the soup, with the already sodden piece of bread threatening to fall into the cup. Her hand was trembling. She couldn't pull her eyes away from his.

She dropped the bread in the soup and pushed it away. The library was mainly dark, the gardens outside giving only a glimmer of deep gold light. But it didn't matter how dim the light was—the only thing she could fixate on right now was him.

His other hand stretched over and tangled in her hair. She sucked in a breath as he stroked the back of her neck. Every part of her skin was tingling.

He moved. It was only one step but he was kissing her, pulling her up into his arms. She wrapped her hands around his neck. Last time he'd kissed her they'd been on the yacht. Tension had been in the air all around them. This time it was different.

This felt like the most natural thing in the world. Every touch of his fingers sent shivers down her spine, building expectation.

This didn't feel as if a man with a kingdom was kissing her. This felt as though *Alex* was kissing her. Alex whom she'd met in Paris all those years ago.

The man she'd watched change over the last few weeks and months. The man who'd taken on board what she'd told him about his child and tried to make changes. He respected her opinion. He'd taken her seriously.

She didn't feel as if she were there as a paid employee any more. It felt like so much more. This felt natural. This felt right. This felt as if it were the place she was supposed to be.

He pulled away and looked down at her. He was smiling. The twinkle in his eyes was back.

'Ruby Wetherspoon...?'

She blinked, not quite sure where this was going. His voice was serious, but the smile hadn't moved from his face. It was almost as if he knew the answer before he asked the question.

'Yes?'

All she could concentrate on right now was the heat of his body against hers. She didn't care that she was wearing ratty clothes. She didn't care that her hair was a mess. All she cared about was the fact she was in Alex's arms.

'Would you do me the honour of coming to Euronia's Annual Charity Ball with me?'

Her throat instantly dried and she wanted to lick her lips. But she couldn't because Alex was kissing her again.

It was almost as if he knew that for a fraction of a second she'd be filled with doubts and he was determined to kiss them away.

This was the first official function he'd invited her to. They'd spent lots of time together—lots of time alone and with Annabelle—but this would be the first time Alex sent a message to the world.

He'd told her he would give her time. And she'd known that he needed time too.

But that time had passed. It felt as if they were both on an even footing. Both in a place where things could develop in the way they wanted.

So she said the thing that felt the most natural to her in the world.

'Yes, Alex. I'd love to.'

# CHAPTER TEN

THE DRESS WAS BEAUTIFUL. More stunning than anything she could have imagined.

Red satin, with a ruched sweetheart bodice encrusted with silver crystals. It hung from the wardrobe door, the crystals glittering and sending sparkles around the room. There were matching silver sandals.

Her stomach was fluttering over and over. Her food tray lay on the table untouched. She couldn't even think about eating.

One of the palace staff had come and set her hair in rollers—a silent girl who'd been ruthlessly efficient: tugging the rollers into place within a few minutes, with strict instructions not to remove them until five minutes before she was ready to leave.

It felt so unreal. Even her face in the mirror looked unreal. The black kohl she occasionally put around her eyes had been smudged uselessly across one cheek. It had taken her two attempts before it looked anything like it should. And the red lipstick seemed too severe. It was a perfect match for her dress—together they would look magnificent—but next to her white skin and dark hair in the bathroom mirror she felt she looked more like the Wicked Queen in *Snow White*.

Doubts were creeping into every corner of her mind. Alex had asked her to come. His reasons seemed valid. But she was just an ordinary girl who knew nothing of visiting dignitaries or the traditions of other countries. At first this had seemed exciting, flattering and little fairytale-ish. Now it seemed terrifying. Every handshake, every nod of her head, every word she said could be wrong.

The last thing she wanted to do was embarrass him.

Maybe things would be better if she stayed in her room?

The door handle creaked and the door edged open. Ruby gasped, her hands automatically going to her bra-covered breasts and her bare abdomen.

But it was Annabelle, dressed in pink pyjamas and with sleepy eyes. She didn't seem the slightest bit concerned to see Ruby half dressed.

'Is something wrong Annabelle?' She knelt on the floor next to the little girl.

But Annabelle's eyes were wide as she looked at the sparkles on the red dress. She let out a little squeak of excitement and pulled her thumb from her mouth, reaching over to touch the dress.

It swung on its hanger, making the sparkles move like little stars in the sky.

The thumb had left a smudge on the delicate fabric, but Ruby didn't care. 'Do you like it, Annabelle?'

The little girl nodded. So Ruby let it swing some

more, sending the sparkles further. She lifted Annabelle into her arms and swung her around, then picked up an abandoned book from the floor.

'Let me take you back to bed,' she said, slipping her arms into her satin dressing gown and padding next door.

She read the caterpillar book until Annabelle fell asleep. She almost wanted to stay there. It would be so much easier falling asleep next to Annabelle than putting on that dress and going out to meet the world.

Alex had asked her to accompany him. What exactly did that mean?

She was Ruby Wetherspoon from Lewisham. She couldn't speak any other languages. She didn't know how to address dignitaries. There was every chance she would seriously offend someone by not shaking their hand the correct way. Her stomach was turning over and over.

Annabelle looked so peaceful. Her attachment to Ruby was growing. It was Ruby she'd seek out now when she was looking for company. It was Ruby she wanted to draw pictures and play games with.

And these last few weeks had brought changes in her demeanour. She wasn't quite so shy. She was gaining confidence. She was interacting better with the children at nursery. She might not be talking, but every day Ruby heard more sounds and expressions. It was almost as if a tiny little valve had been released and she was becoming more comfortable.

Last night Ruby had been convinced that the humming along to *Finding Nemo* was becoming a murmur. She'd been careful not to react. She'd stayed exactly where she was, letting Annabelle lie in her arms until she'd fallen asleep and then gently sliding her arms out from underneath her.

The thought of going away and leaving this little girl was starting to play on her mind. The hospital in the UK had started to ask her for the date of her return. It seemed reasonable. She hadn't expected to be here this long. But the days had quickly turned into weeks, and the weeks into months. Euronia was starting to feel like home—no matter how many times Polly phoned her and told her it was time to return to London.

She wasn't sure she wanted to leave Annabelle.

She wasn't sure she wanted to leave Alex.

Where had *that* come from?

Her face flushed and she walked back into her own room, shedding her dressing gown and pulling the red dress from the hanger and stepping into it.

She sucked in her breath and slid the zip up at the back. It fitted perfectly—just like everything the palace had provided. The silver sandals were elegant, but comfortable. The only thing missing was jewellery.

Nothing really suited. Her plain gold earrings and chain looked paltry next to the designer gown. Maybe it would be better with nothing at all?

She smiled at her reflection in the mirror. With

the rollers removed her dark hair was hanging in curls, covering her shoulders. The boning and the crystals on the dress gave her a more curvaceous shape than normal. And now, with the dress in place, her skin didn't look quite so pale or her lips so red.

Her hands trembled as she took off her gold earrings.

Tonight she was going to a ball in the palace.

Tonight she was going to a ball with her own prince.

Just for tonight she might actually be a princess.

Just for tonight she might actually look as if she was worthy of Alex.

And tonight, for the first time, she might actually feel as if she was part of a couple—even if it was only in her head.


Alex had been pacing for the last thirty minutes, wondering when Ruby would appear.

The palace was buzzing. It had been over a year since there had been a ball at the palace. When his mother and father had ruled there had been several balls every year, all raising money for various charities.

Alex had given some instructions on which charities he wanted to support, and the various people he wanted to invite. But all the details had been dealt with by his staff.

In less than a few minutes over a thousand people

would be in the palace. He had guards in all corridors, letting the guests know which areas were open to the public and which were not. The corridor that held Ruby and Annabelle certainly wasn't.

He walked along its length, cursing himself for not saying goodnight to Annabelle earlier. He opened her door just a crack—she was already sleeping, her book and a stuffed caterpillar beside her on the bed.

He walked across the room and dropped a kiss on her forehead before quietly closing the door behind him. His fingers tightened around the black velvet box in his hands. He was still unsure. This felt right—he just didn't know how Ruby would react.

He knocked on her door before he could change his mind.

She opened the door and met him with a smile. 'Hi, Alex. What do you think?'

There was a tremor in her voice. An uncertainty.

He couldn't speak. He must have the dopiest smile on his face right now. What did he *think*? She'd just blown him away!

Ruby was always gorgeous—usually understated, but gorgeous nonetheless. But he'd never seen Ruby the grown-up.

The scarlet dress was stunning. Elegant without giving anything way. Hugging her curves but sweeping the floor and keeping everything covered. The beads along her bodice sparkled in the dim evening light snaking through the windows.

Her hair had been styled into large curls, covering her bare shoulders. She was wearing more make-up than usual, but it was perfect. Highlighting her flawless skin, dark brown eyes and red lips.

He held out the black box towards her. 'You look *almost* perfect, Ruby.'

'Almost?'

It was obvious she knew he was teasing her. She stepped forward, reaching out for the box.

He could tell she was nervous—her hands were trembling slightly. Would she know he was nervous too?

She lifted the lid and let out a little gasp. The diamonds were dazzling. The jewels on her dress paled in comparison to these. He knew instantly he'd done the right thing.

'Alex…' Her eyes were wide. 'Where did these come from?' She held up one of the earrings, its thirty hanging diamonds bright and clear.

'They were my mother's. I knew you were nervous about tonight. I thought it might be nice if you had something of hers to wear.'

'You want me to wear *these*?' She looked almost terrified. 'But they must be worth a fortune.' Her fingers went automatically to her earlobe. 'What if I lose one?'

He shook his head and smiled. 'You won't. Don't worry.'

'But—'

'But nothing.' He spun her around to face the

full-length mirror in the room and held up one of the earrings next to her ear. 'Can't you see how perfect it looks?'

She could hardly argue. Her face said exactly how she was feeling.

She put her hand up over her heart. 'They're beautiful. They set off the dress perfectly.' She turned around towards him. 'How did you know?'

'Because my mother had impeccable taste, Ruby. It wouldn't have mattered what you wore tonight—these earrings were always going to be a perfect match.' He bent a little lower and whispered in her ear. 'You have a lot in common with her.'

'What does that mean?'

'It means that you look beautiful.' He pressed the earrings into her hand. 'Here—put them on and let's go.'

She stood in front of the mirror, putting the earrings in place, then stopped for a second to study her reflection. She was trying to calm herself. Trying to steady herself for the night ahead.

He put his arms on her shoulders. 'You're going to be the most beautiful woman in the room, Ruby Wetherspoon.'

He was standing by her shoulder, looking at their reflection in the glass. He knew she was nervous. He was nervous himself. Although this was meant to be a private function, nothing could ever really be private when a thousand people were involved.

This would be the first time since Sophia had

died that he'd officially invited someone to be his partner. He was well aware of how some of his guests might react. But the charity ball had always been an informal occasion. In a way, it might give Ruby a taste of what could lie ahead.

He hadn't even broached that question with her on the yacht. There had been too much more to deal with. But now the time was right.

He slid his hand into hers. 'Are you ready? Because you look beautiful.'

She nodded slowly and touched the glittering diamonds in her ears. 'I'm ready now.' She sounded more confident. More sure.

He didn't have a shadow of a doubt. His mother would have loved Ruby Wetherspoon.

The first disaster was tripping over her dress. Even though it was gorgeous, and made-to-measure, she wasn't standing quite as straight as she should be. As a result the bottom seam of the dress kept catching on her toes.

A strong hand at her elbow stopped her face-planting on the floor. At first she thought it was Alex, but he was on her other side. A quick glance proved it to be one of the waiters, with a whole silver tray of canapés in his other hand.

He gave her a little conspiratorial nod. 'Mind your step, m'lady.'

She gathered up part of the dress in her hand. Her stomach was turning over and over. Another waiter proffered a tray with champagne flutes but she shook her head—champagne was the last thing she needed right now.

Alex turned and smiled at her. It was the first time she'd really seen him in formal dress. He'd been pressed up behind her next to the mirror, and she'd been so dazzled by the diamonds that she hadn't noticed how handsome he looked. The black dress uniform suited him perfectly, with its sweeping red sash across his chest and adorned with several gold medals.

It hadn't even occurred to her that the sash was the exact same red as her dress. Had Alex done that deliberately?

They walked through the ballroom doors side by side. It wasn't so bad. There was no audible hush when they appeared, just a few quiet gestures and murmurs.

Alex immediately went into charm mode—working the room and talking to lots of the guests, his arm behind her, gently guiding her from person to person. Sometimes he spoke in French, sometimes in German. After the first few words she was mainly lost, and just nodded and smiled along, shaking a proffered hand when appropriate.

The diamonds had felt dazzling in her ears upstairs—if a little ostentatious—but in this room it was clear that Ruby was the least adorned woman there. Everywhere she turned there were rings the size of rocks and twinkling tiaras.

She'd recognised a few faces from royal families across Europe, all in dazzling jewels. And even the movie stars and supermodels were adorned with diamond necklaces and bracelets.

A blonde actress—one of her favourites—was right in front of her. She was immaculate, as usual, in a figure-hugging black dress high at the neck but with virtually no back. How she kept the dress in place was a mystery to Ruby.

She spun on her heels and tilted her head, unashamedly studying Ruby. Waves of discomfort washed over her, along with a distinct flow of blood to the cheeks. She was determined not to be intimidated.

She held out her hand. 'Maria Cochette? It's a pleasure to meet you. I'm Ruby Wetherspoon.'

Her hand stayed in the air for the longest time.

'I know who you are.'

The Italian accent that sounded so cute on screen was harsh in real life. Maria's eyes swept up and down Ruby with obvious distaste. The dress that had felt so perfect upstairs suddenly felt old-fashioned and overdone.

This was a woman who had charmed in every interview Ruby had ever watched. She exuded elegance and grace. But the look she was giving Ruby now held none of those things.

She moved closer, still ignoring Ruby's outstretched hand. Her voice lowered. 'So how did you do it? How did little Plain Jane manage to catch the

Prince's eye?' She sneered. 'Or was it just too easy for him to do the hired help?' The vulgar words were spat out. 'Lydia Merr told me about you. She said you weren't even eye candy—and she was right.'

Ruby had never been a girl for conflict. But if she'd been any other place, at any other time, she would have punched the perfect Maria clean in the face. Alex had warned her that Mrs Merr was a renowned gossip, and it seemed their kiss hadn't gone unnoticed.

For the first time that night she drew herself up to her full height. She almost felt her dress lift from the floor. Up close, Maria wasn't so perfect. Botox had made her eyebrows arch unevenly. Her suntanned skin couldn't hide the wrinkles around her eyes.

Ruby lifted her hand up to her ears and smiled sweetly, though she knew her eyes would be shooting daggers. She'd dealt with too many difficult patients and members of staff over the years to simper around a woman like this.

'I guess some of us have hidden talents, Maria. Or maybe our core values and ethics are just apparent.' She let her fingers run over the sparkling drop diamonds. 'Do you like the earrings Alex gave me to wear? They were his mother's.'

The diamonds were elegant, in contrast; the bling from Maria was almost blinding her.

She met the cold grey eyes with another smile. 'I always think that less is more, don't you?'

She didn't wait for an answer—just turned and walked away, ignoring the stifled noise of indignation behind her.

Ruby never behaved like that. But something had burned inside her. Was it the way Maria had looked at Alex? Or her total disrespect for Ruby?

Her stomach flipped over. Would this be something she would need to get used to?

She almost stumbled over her feet. Where had *that* thought come from? This was their first official outing together. It might lead to nothing.

But all of a sudden, even after all their talks and all this time, Ruby felt woefully unprepared. Alex had said nothing to her, but this almost felt like a test to see how she would do. A test she was about to fail spectacularly if her exchange with Maria was anything to go on.

She looked around the room. She didn't have a single friend here.

It was a sobering thought.

And all of a sudden she felt very alone. When was the last time she'd spoken to Polly?

She was planning on spending Christmas with her parents in France—that was only a few weeks away—but for the first time since she'd got here she missed her colleagues, she missed her friends, she missed her flat.

It was this. It was here—standing in this room with hundreds of people and the only person who had her back was Alex.

It was as if he felt the vibe across the room. He looked up and his gaze met hers, and he gave her a quizzical are-you-all-right? look. It was impossible, but she felt as if she could see the bright blue of his eyes even from this distance.

He started to walk towards her and her feet automatically moved in response. All she could do was smile. It didn't matter who else was in the room. The only person who mattered was Alex. And he was looking at her as if he felt exactly the same way.

The voices, the jewels, the chatter all around her just faded to background noise. Her smile was getting broader by the second. It was the strongest urge, the greatest pull she'd ever felt. Like metal being drawn towards a magnet from a million miles away.

Several people tried to talk to him as he made his way towards her, but Alex didn't even blink— he just kept his eyes focused entirely on her.

Seconds later he filled her entire view. For another second both of them hesitated. Then his arms were around her waist, her hands were resting on his shoulders.

'Are you okay?'

'I am now.'

She'd never felt more sure of anything. This time there *was* a hush in the room. Their actions had attracted everyone's attention.

But Alex's bright blue eyes were still fixed on hers. 'You're the most beautiful woman in the room, Ruby.'

His voice was low, for her ears only.

'That's the way I always feel around you,' she murmured.

'Good.'

His lips met hers. She could hear the audible gasps around her but she didn't care. Alex was kissing in her in front of everyone. Alex was making his intentions clear.

It was as if she could soar. Soar above the shocked faces in the ballroom and soar above the pink palace. The kiss in Paris had been special—had been electric—but this kiss was everything. He spun her around as he kissed her and they both started to laugh. Knowing entirely how it looked.

He pulled his lips back, their noses still touching. 'You're mine, Ruby Wetherspoon. And the whole world knows it.'

'And you're mine right back.'

She'd never thought she'd say those words. She'd never thought she'd believe them. But this moment was hers. Hers and Alex's.

'I don't really want to look around,' she said. 'I don't want anyone to spoil what's happening between us.'

His eyes were still fixed on her face. He was smiling. 'Who could do that?'

It was almost as if a gong had sounded. Some ancient clanging noise reverberating around the room. But it was actually the opposite.

Silence. Pure and utter silence.

No one was talking. No one was murmuring. All she could hear was her and Alex breathing. Every tiny hair on her arms stood on end. It was as if someone were walking over her grave.

'Alex?'

He looked up and his hands dropped from her waist. There was an elderly couple standing in the doorway. Immaculately regal. Both were staring at Alex.

It took her a few seconds. She'd never met or seen pictures of Sophia's parents. But for a reaction like this it had to be them.

She glanced nervously at Alex. How much had they seen? Had they seen him kiss her, or just hold her?

Those few seconds whilst he gathered himself seemed to stretch into hours. She saw everything. The fleeting moment of panic followed by the worry of what to do next.

Her heart plummeted. He'd been carried away. He hadn't thought of the consequences of kissing her in front of everyone. This was a disaster.

Every eye in the room flicked between them and Sophia's parents.

She heard Alex suck in a deep breath, then his hand moved over and took hers.

The feeling of skin against skin was unexpected. Her gaze fixed on their hands as he intertwined their fingers. He moved forward in long strides and she struggled to keep up, having to gather her dress in her hand to stop it from tangling around her feet again.

He gave a courteous bow to the King and Queen. 'Ruby Wetherspoon, I'd like you to meet Annabelle's grandparents—King Henry and Queen Isabelle of Leruna.'

Her brain was racing. What on earth would they think of her?

There were a few expanding seconds of silence. Then their immaculate breeding kicked into place.

The King gave a nod of his head, 'Ms Wetherspoon.'

The Queen took a little longer. But her wide-eyed look had disappeared. Ruby could almost tell that to this woman composure was everything.

She held out a hand towards her. Ruby felt a second of panic—was she supposed to shake it or kiss it?

Alex made the tiniest movement and she reached out and shook the Queen's hand. Something from fairytales long ago made her curtsy. 'It's a pleasure to meet you, Queen Isabelle.'

As she stood up it was clear the Queen was regarding her carefully. Her heart was fluttering madly in her chest. If she didn't calm down soon she'd end up in a crumpled heap on the floor. She felt as if the whole room was watching her. Anything she did right now would be crucial. Her actions and demeanour would temper what everyone in the room thought of her.

It was as if a lightbulb had gone off in her head. All of a sudden she realised just how much of a chance Alex had taken on her.

She sucked in a breath. She was worthy. She was worthy of his faith in her. She just had to show it.

She was still holding the Queen's hand, and Isabelle's eyes were starting to smart with disapproval.

Despite her glittering tiara and her sumptuous silver gown, Ruby knew a clear way to connect with this woman. In her job she'd managed to charm the most difficult family members over the last ten years, and she could do it again now.

'It's been a pleasure to work with Annabelle these last few months. She's such a wonderful little girl and she's making real progress.'

Isabelle looked a little startled at the familiarity. People probably didn't speak to her like this. But as soon as Annabelle's name was mentioned it was clear she was interested.

'You're the speech therapist.' There was just the slightest hint of distaste—as if she were trying to put Ruby in her place.

'She's my friend.' Alex's words were quiet, but firm. Shooting a crystal-clear message across the tension-laden air. It was like a subtle counter-attack.

But this woman with decades of experience didn't even blink. Her eyebrows rose a little. 'Progress? Is she starting to talk?'

She was clearly surprised.

Ruby nodded and moved closer to her, away from

the prying ears that were straining all around the room to hear their conversation.

Alex shot her a look that was a cross between pure relief and pleading, and with an almost imperceptible nod engaged the King in conversation, leading him over towards a drinks tray.

Ruby held out her hand to let the Queen lead the direction of their steps, and was unsurprised to find her leading them towards the entrance to another room filled with antique mahogany chairs. The door was closed quickly behind them by one of the palace attendants.

The Queen settled herself in one of the chairs and arranged her skirts around her before gesturing to Ruby to sit down too.

'Tell me about Annabelle.'

Ruby smiled. 'I've seen definite progress in the last few months. It's slow. But steady. I don't dispute the diagnosis of selective mutism. But do you know that in some cases children will speak in some circumstances but not others?'

The Queen gave the smallest of nods, so Ruby continued. 'Annabelle was silent when I got here. Over the last weeks and month we've noticed noises.'

'Noises?'

'Yes. Gasps of excitement. Whoops of pleasure. Whimpers when we're watching scary movies.'

'My granddaughter *whoops*?' There was an amused edge to her voice.

'Yes, she does. But that's not all—she often hums along to some of the songs in her favourite films. She seems to do it quite unconsciously—usually when she's most relaxed or when she's tired.'

'And she's that way around *you*?' The timbre of the Queen's voice had changed slightly.

'It's taken her a while to get to know me,' said Ruby quickly. 'But she's been spending more time with her father.'

Part of her wondered if she should be saying this. She didn't want to make it sound as if Alex had neglected Annabelle in any way at all.

'We've made sure that all the palace staff knows that his time with Annabelle is to be uninterrupted. It's time they spend alone—together.'

She was starting to get nervous and her mouth was running away from her. She wanted to be clear that she wasn't trying to push herself between Alex and his daughter. The last thing she wanted was for the Queen to think she was trying to take Sophia's place.

'And is this working?' There was a tone of slight disbelief. As if she didn't quite understand the significance.

'It's definitely working. Annabelle is changing. Her confidence has increased in leaps and bounds. She's a different little girl than the one I met when I arrived.'

For the smallest of seconds—almost instinctively—the Queen's eyes narrowed. She straightened herself in her chair, pulling herself up to her full height. 'Why do you think my granddaughter doesn't talk, Ms Wetherspoon?'

There was a whole host of things she could say here. But experience had taught her to go with her instinct.

'I think she misses her mother,' she said simply.

There was the tiniest sound. A little gasp from the Queen. Then the woman's eyes clouded, as if they were fogged by impending tears.

It was the clearest and most confident Ruby had felt all evening. Isabelle might be a distinguished queen—something that was way out of Ruby's realm of expertise—but she was also a concerned grandmother—something Ruby *could* understand.

Ruby leaned over and squeezed her hand, and then changed position, gathering her dress and kneeling in front of the Queen.

'Science tells us that even babies can form memories. Annabelle heard and recognised her mother's voice for nine months in the womb, and then for another eleven months after she was born.' She let go of the skirts in her hand and pressed her other hand over her heart. 'She remembers her mother in *here*.'

Her voice was becoming huskier. She wasn't trying to upset the Queen, but she felt it was important to be honest with her.

'Alex has put a picture of Sophia next to Annabelle's bed. He has made a picture album with photos of the two of them—as children they almost look like twins. It has pictures of Sophia alone, and pictures of her with Annabelle.' She squeezed the Queen's hand again. 'He talks about her every night with Annabelle.'

If the Queen disapproved of Ruby using the familiar form of Alex's name she didn't show it. A slow tear trickled down her cheek. 'He does?'

Ruby nodded. 'It's not sad. It's not morbid. He just tells her a little story—something about her mother—and they move on to something else. They play a game. Watch some TV together.'

The older woman's lips were trembling. 'And who has helped him to do that?'

Isabelle's pale grey eyes were fixed on hers. Ruby took a deep breath. 'I have. Everything about their relationship has changed. I think Alex had a lot of grief locked up inside. Talking and spending time with his daughter has helped them both.'

The Queen's gaze was fixed on Ruby. 'You did this? You did this for them?'

A flash of recognition crossed her eyes, along with a whole host of fleeting emotions.

Ruby could step back at this point. She could fall into professional mode. It would keep her safe. It would keep her guarded. But the Queen had already seen Alex's arms around her. Maybe she had seen more. It was time for honesty.

'I care about them. I care about them both very much.'

The Queen licked her lips. 'Do you think my granddaughter will ever talk?'

'I can't say for sure—but I do think so. I think she spoke the other day at nursery. I think she might have said something to one of the other children. But I didn't want to make a scene. I didn't want to draw her attention to the fact. We all have to be patient.'

'And are *you* patient, Ruby Wetherspoon?'

The question shocked her. It might sound simple, but the Queen clearly wasn't talking about Annabelle's speech any more. She meant something else entirely.

Was she brave enough to be honest?

*I've waited ten years* were the words on her lips.

'I am.'

There were another few moments' silence. It was almost as if the Queen were taking time to digest all she'd told her. She shifted a little closer to the edge of the chair—a little closer to Ruby.

'Alexander was Sophia's safe place.'

Her voice was shaky, but controlled. Her silver-grey eyes were fixed on Ruby's.

'He was the one person she trusted to give her the ultimate gift.'

Ruby's stomach squeezed. It would always hurt. It would always reach little parts of her that she couldn't share.

Her voice was shaking too. 'Annabelle is a beautiful gift. Of that there is no doubt.'

Their eyes met again and she felt the common understanding between them. This woman had lost her precious daughter. Her life would never be the same again.

If she wanted to she could hate Ruby. She could make life difficult for Alex. She could make their relationship impossible.

But it seemed she had no wish to do that.

'I'm glad my granddaughter has someone who has her best interests at heart. I'm glad that Alexander is looking to build a life for himself and his daughter again.'

She pushed herself up from the chair and gave a little nod to Ruby with the hint of a smile.

'And I would very much like to hear my granddaughter speak.'

Ruby straightened up and her knees gave an unexpected crack. She let out a nervous laugh—it certainly displaced any anxiety in the room.

Queen Isabelle gave her a serene smile. 'I'm tired. But if I retired for the evening now people would talk. We should return to the ballroom together. I'll be able to leave after a while.'

Ruby nodded. Of course. People had seen them leave the ballroom together and their tongues would wag if they didn't return together.

Then the Queen did something she didn't expect. She held out her elbow towards Ruby. An invitation to take it. Before it had been polite and because they were in company. In the confines of this room, when it was just the two of them, it was something she didn't have to do.

Ruby didn't hesitate. She slid her arm next to the Queen's and joined her in walking towards the door.

Isabelle's smile had stayed on her face. 'Beautiful earrings, Ms Wetherspoon. They seem familiar. Queen Marguerite had exquisite taste, didn't she?'

Ruby's heart squeezed inside her chest. *She knew.* She knew Alex had given them to her to wear this evening.

They walked through the door arm in arm.

The glass doors from the ballroom leading out to the gardens were open, letting the cool fresh air sweep in. Ten years ago New Year's Eve in Paris had been cold, but winter in Euronia was much warmer. People drifted in and out of the ballroom and the gardens as the music played.

People were curious about her now. Alex appeared by her side every ten minutes or so, introducing her to diplomats and other royals. They shook her hand and gave her guarded smiles. The celebrity guests were much more up-front. Apart from her earlier encounter with Maria Cochette, everyone else seemed to want to be her new best friend. It was odd. Perhaps it was the fact that Alex had kissed her in front of everyone. His message had been clear.

The scene that everyone had expected in front of Sophia's parents hadn't materialised. When she'd re-entered the ballroom on the arm of Queen Isabelle some mouths had dropped open. Even Alex had looked a bit shocked, but he'd covered it well.

His hands had appeared at her waist a little later and his mouth at her ear. 'What did you do?' he whispered.

'I told the truth,' she said simply, and he'd twirled her around in the next dance.

The evening passed by in a flash. She didn't even notice when the King and Queen of Leruna slipped away—she was too busy focusing on Alex.

He was more attentive than ever, leaving her in no doubt of his attentions. Every tiny brush of his fingertips on her skin ignited the fire within her. Every time he caught her eye, or gave her a smile from across the room, she felt as if she were the only person there.

When finally the last person left her feet were throbbing and her jaw was aching from smiling so much.

Alex appeared at her side and took the champagne glass from her hand. 'Are you tired?'

She shook her head. 'No. I don't want this night to end.'

He took her hand in his and led her up the huge curved staircase and along the corridor towards his rooms. Their footsteps quickened as they walked, their anticipation building.

He swung the door of his apartment wide. She'd never been in here before. Alex had always been around her and Annabelle in their rooms, or in the main parts of the palace. She'd had no reason to visit his rooms.

The room was stark. Different from the other very ornate rooms in the palace.

No antique furniture. No sumptuous furnishings. It was white and black—like a modern apartment in the middle of New York—certainly not what she expected to find in a pink palace.

'Alex?'

She turned to face him and her heart squeezed at the expression on his face. These were the rooms he'd shared with his wife. He didn't need to say anything. Everything in this room had been stripped bare—just like his heart. She understood in a heartbeat.

She closed the door quietly behind her and stepped over to him. 'Oh, Alex...'

She ran her fingers through his hair as he closed his eyes.

Everything—all their conversations—had been about *her* being ready. But the truth was it was about *him* being ready too.

Part of this was painful. Because after tonight she'd never been more sure about what she wanted. It was Alex. It had always been Alex. It would always be Alex.

But did he really want her? Or was she just someone to plug the gap his wife had left?

It should unsettle her that these were the rooms he'd shared with his wife. It should make her feel uncomfortable. But she had a feeling that there wasn't a single part of Sophia left in here.

Her fingers were still running through his hair— his hands were planted firmly on her hips. She stepped closer to him and placed a gentle kiss on the soft skin at the side of his neck.

'Are you ready for this, Alex? Are you ready for us?'

Every knot inside him was beginning to unravel. He'd held himself in check all night. From the first second he'd seen Ruby in her red dress he'd wanted to have her in this position. She was everything to him. And now he was finally free to say it—finally free to let the world know.

The arrival of Sophia's parents had been more than unexpected. They were always invited to formal occasions at the palace. But since Sophia's death they'd never attended.

They saw Annabelle on regular occasions, but they were always private times.

He'd been horrified when they'd arrived—horrified that their first view of Ruby was in his arms with his mouth on hers.

With a few hours' hindsight he realised that Queen Isabelle must have heard through the grapevine about Ruby. They'd attended with the sole reason of meeting the woman who might replace their daughter in his affections.

Isabelle had always known the truth of their relationship and their marriage. But she'd supported them both every step of the way. She'd once told Alex that there were lots of forms of love. Some with fireworks, some with steady steps, and some with bonds of loyalty that would forsake all others.

The King had mentioned nothing of Ruby at all. He'd spoken to Alex at length about business worries and difficult negotiations.

When Alex had watched Ruby and Queen Isabelle leave the room together he'd felt sick. *Should he intervene?* But he'd been almost sure that Ruby wouldn't want that.

And when they'd returned some time later Queen Isabelle had been serenely graceful, as always, when she'd told Alex that Ruby seemed like 'a nice girl'.

His sense of relief had been enormous.

And now here they were. In the one place he'd wanted to bring her all night.

'I've been ready for ten years, Ruby,' he whispered in her ear. 'I've waited a long time for this.'

'Me too.'

Her brown eyes were fixed on his. Just like that night in Paris. The only thing missing was the reflection of the fireworks.

Ruby… Every bit as beautiful as she'd been ten years ago. Those brown eyes seemed to pull him right in, touching his heart and his soul. For the first time in ten years he was free to love exactly who he wanted to love. He had the strength and the power of his convictions and he knew what was right for him and what was right for his child. *Who* was right for him and who was right for Annabelle.

Ruby might not be Annabelle's mother, but her patience and affection for his little girl was clear. Their relationship had changed exponentially. Ruby spent hours playing with her, not just assessing the little girl. Trust had built between them. When Annabelle smiled at Ruby and looked at her in that way she had, it made his heart melt.

His little girl was every bit as much in love with Ruby as he was.

He ran his fingers along her velvet skin, from her fingertips to her shoulders. She gave a little shudder of pleasure as she smiled at him. When his fingers reached her shoulders he swept one hand along the back of her neck and traced the other gently across her décolletage. His fingers stopped mid-point as she closed her eyes and swayed a little. The curve of her breasts was highlighted in the figure-hugging dress. If Ruby knew who'd actually designed it for her, and how much it had cost, she would probably be horrified.

His hands joined at the back of the dress, where he caught the zipper in his fingers and started to release it slowly. She was holding her breath as he inched it lower. The shimmering red fabric slid from her frame and puddled on the floor at her feet as he tangled his fingers in her hair and pulled her against him.

Kissing Ruby before had been tantalising. Magical. Full of expectations and promise.

Kissing Ruby in his room as he shucked off his jacket and trousers was more than he could ever have imagined. He walked backwards, pulling her with him as they sank down on to the white bed.

The eiderdown enveloped them both. He'd dreamed about this for the last ten years. But the reality was far more incredible than his imagination could ever have envisaged. And he could envisage quite a bit.

He pulled his lips back for a second as his fingers brushed against her underwear. 'Are you sure about this, Ruby? Because there's no going back. This has to be right for both of us.'

She was holding her breath again, fixing him with her chocolate eyes. His fingers danced along her silky-smooth skin.

Her perfect red lips broke into a smile as she pressed against him. 'This is right, Alex. This has *always* been right.'

And then she kissed him again and he forgot about everything else.

# CHAPTER ELEVEN

PEOPLE WERE LOOKING at her. People were fixing their eyes on her and muttering under their breath. She'd been in the shops in the city centre on lots of occasions recently but she'd never noticed this.

Even Pierre in the baker's shop wasn't his usual friendly self. He hardly even made eye contact before he handed her a brown paper bag of baked goods and waved his hand at her attempt at payment.

It made her feel uneasy. She might not speak fluent French, but she'd always muddled through and felt welcome in Euronia before.

This morning had been so strange.

The thing that she'd secretly dreamed about for such a long time had finally come true. Waking up in Alex's arms had been fantastic.

Stealing along the corridor with her dress clutched around her hadn't been quite so fantastic. But she hadn't been sure if any of the staff—in particular Rufus—might routinely go into Alex's room to wake him.

There was still so much about the palace protocols she had to learn. And last night she hadn't thought to ask Alex about any of these things—

there had been far too many other sensations occupying her mind.

It had seemed so much easier to duck out and get back to her room to shower and dress. But once she'd got ready her stomach had begun churning again.

On one hand she'd wanted to go back to Alex's room. On the other she'd wanted to give him a little space. And yet they had to talk about what would happen next. About Annabelle. About Sophia's parents. All the things they hadn't really focused on last night when they'd been in each other's arms.

She loved him. She was sure of it. She just hadn't told him yet.

Maybe tonight they would be able to re-enact the whole thing. Maybe she could tell him then. But the truth was as soon as Alex had started kissing her everything else had gone out of the window except the feel of his body pressed against hers. The touch of his fingers on her skin. The sensation of his lips on her neck…

The newspapers outside one of the nearby shops fluttered in the wind. Something caught her attention. It was the colour on the front page. The exact colour of one of the dresses in her wardrobe back at the palace.

Her feet were drawn automatically. Her hand was pushing back the fluttering pages.

*Princess Ruby?*

The words leapt out at her and she jumped backwards on the pavement. *No. It couldn't say that.* Her heart was pounding in her chest. What on earth…?

She stepped forward again. Pushing the front page back and scanning the page. It was totally in French. She couldn't understand what was written at all.

But she really didn't need to understand. The picture said it all.

It must have been taken a few months before—just after she'd arrived. She and Alex were sitting at the café and her bright pink dress was fluttering around her—just as the newspaper pages were doing today.

But it was the moment that the picture had captured. That second when Alex had leaned forward and cradled her cheek. He was looking at her as though she was the only person in the world and she was looking at him exactly the same way.

That moment had literally been the blink of an eye. A tiny, private fragment of two lives captured for eternity for the world.

And it had changed everything.

It was printed alongside a picture from the ball. Ruby in her long red dress with diamonds glittering in her ears.

Some eagle-eyed journalist had found and printed a picture of Alex's mother wearing the same earrings years earlier.

She couldn't understand any of the words that

were written. But she could understand the panic clamouring in her chest.

*No.* Just when things between her and Alex seemed to be heading in a perfect direction.

What was happening between them was private. It wasn't for the world's consumption. She felt indignant. She felt angry. She felt stupid.

Alex was a prince—at some point would be King. This would always be the life of whoever he showed interest in. She was a fool to think otherwise. And this was exactly what he'd tried to warn her about.

She leaned back against the newspaper rack, breathing heavily. She was seeing tiny stars in her peripheral vision. People were staring at her and whispering. Her phone started to ring and she grappled with her bag to pull it out.

It was a number she didn't recognise. 'Hello?'

'Ruby Wetherspoon? This is Frank Barnes from *Celebrity News*. We'd like to interview you.'

'How did you get this number? This is a private number.'

'We'd like to know about your relationship with the Prince Regent and the recent photos that have been taken of the two of you together. We understand that you're working together. But it looks a whole lot more personal than that. Would you like to do an exclusive with us?'

Every word sent a chill down her body. For a few

seconds she couldn't even speak. Then, 'No. Don't phone again.'

She disconnected the call and looked around her. Alex. She had to talk to Alex.

Her phone started to ring again. Another unknown number. She pressed the button at the top, switching the whole thing off.

She put her head down and her legs on automatic pilot, walking back to the palace. She resisted the temptation to break into a run.

The warm sun was usually pleasant, but her face felt flushed and she could feel the sweat running down her back. The usually enticing smells from the delicatessen, the baker and chocolatier made her stomach flip over.

All she wanted to do was talk to someone—talk to Alex. Talk to Polly. Talk to anyone—anyone but a journalist.

Her legs were burning. The warm air didn't seem to be fully filling her lungs. There it was in the distance—the pink palace. She reached the gates and crossed the gardens quickly. The driveway had never seemed so long.

When she finally reached the palace entrance the doorman barely glanced at her. Was that a sign of something?

As she stepped into the hallway she was aware of the absolute silence. Usually there was always noise from somewhere—talking servants, discussions between visitors, footsteps from people going about their daily business.

Today the whole palace seemed silent.

She turned on her heel and headed for the library. If she'd had an ounce of common sense about her she would have purchased one of those newspapers. Instead she was reduced to doing an internet search.

The amount of hits made her cringe. *How many?*

Her eyes widened as she read, and tears formed in her eyes as a horrible feeling of dread crept over her skin.

Pictures really did speak a thousand words.

If Alex had any doubt about how she felt about him, once he'd glanced at these pictures he—and the world—would know for sure.

If she was an ordinary girl, in an ordinary world, this might seem quite nice. The looks and glances in the pictures were reciprocal. She wasn't just fawning over him. Their gazes were locked together—as if, for that second, they were the only two people on the planet.

Little moments, captured in time.

Tears started to roll down her cheeks. She'd tried to be so careful. She'd tried to be guarded. She didn't want the whole world to know that she'd loved Alex de Castellane for the last ten years. It had taken her long enough to admit that to herself.

Things were good between them right now. Things were great. Annabelle was showing real signs of improvement. And Alex...

He was showing real signs of moving on. *Really* moving on.

Last night had been wonderful.

She clicked on another link. This time it was a red-top newspaper from England. It carried the same photographs as the others. But the text took her breath away.

Vitriol. Libel.

Ruby Wetherspoon had been plotting to get her hands on Alex de Castellane for years. She'd come to Euronia purely with the purpose of trapping the world's most eligible bachelor into marriage. She was a devious woman with money on her mind.

No mention of Annabelle. No mention of her job.

She clicked on the next link. An exclusive from Maria Cochette, telling of how Ruby Wetherspoon had laughed at the way she'd tricked Alex into giving her his mother's diamond earrings and said it was only a matter of time before she got a whole lot more. Apparently Maria had known right from the start what kind of woman she was—and Alex was still heartbroken after the death of his wife... he was vulnerable.

Ruby retched. Any minute now she was going to be sick.

This was all her own fault. She should never have crossed Maria Cochette last night. Of *course* someone like her would have newspaper contacts. The truth was Ruby had no idea how to handle people like that. She was unprepared for what she was up against—and it showed. She just wasn't equipped to be part of this world.

The tiny little bit of backbone she'd shown last night had backfired spectacularly.

How many times had she picked up a newspaper or a glossy magazine and devoured all the headline news? She'd read about affairs, arguments, secret children, kidnapping, celebrity diets and drunken parties. Although she was sure it was sometimes blown out of proportion, she'd never really given much thought as to how much of it was actually lies.

She'd never given *any* thought to the fact that some of those people might be hurt by what was being written about them. She'd never considered it at all.

Not until now.

It seemed some of the papers had gone to extremes. One had tracked down an ex-boyfriend for a whole range of quotes about her that had been blown out of proportion.

She cringed. Luke wasn't that kind of guy. He wasn't malicious and she knew that. He'd just been blind-sided. But the words *'I always knew she wouldn't stay with me'* still hurt.

The truth was Luke had never really stood a chance against the memory of a guy he knew nothing about. None of her exes ever had.

She was feeling swamped. Overwhelmed. No one mentioned the kiss. No one mentioned the fact that

Alex had kissed her in front of everyone and made it clear how he felt about her.

Maria Cochette claimed she'd hung over Alex all night—apparently her conduct had been 'desperate and embarrassing'.

Other reports said the King and Queen of Leruna had been 'horrified' by her presence and had seemingly reacted with shock at the thought of Princess Ruby replacing their daughter.

Was this true? Had she maybe misread the whole situation?

Right now she didn't know what was right and what was wrong.

Her eyes swam with tears. Reaction was overwhelming her, swamping her with emotions she didn't know how to control.

Today should be a happy day. Today should be the start of a new kind of relationship with Alex.

Instead it was turning into the worst day of her life, with the world thinking she was some kind of sad, desperate woman who wanted to trap a prince.

Not a girl whose heart was filled with joy because she'd finally connected with the man she'd loved for ten years.

There was a noise behind her. Alex. His face was almost grey and the warm eyes she'd expected to see were clouded with worry. Rufus and another advisor were at his back.

'There you are, Ruby.' He walked across the library in long strides. 'We need to talk.'

Today wasn't supposed to be like this. He was supposed to be smiling. Taking her in his arms and telling her that he loved her.

But Alex looked distant.

She could almost see all her hopes and dreams disintegrating in front of her.

This was all her nightmares come true.

For a few seconds that morning everything had been perfect—right up until he'd woken up and found his bed empty.

Ruby was gone. He'd expected her still to be in his arms, expected to touch her soft hair and stroke her silky skin. Instead there had been a little dip in the bed where she'd lain.

He hadn't had much time to think after that, because Rufus and the other advisors had arrived, their faces grim.

It had been more than bad news. Ruby had been painted as a villain across the world's media. He guessed that jealous Maria Cochette had phoned most of her contacts to give the most skewed and inaccurate view of the evening.

His worst fears. People had painted his marriage to Sophia as a fairytale. No woman could live up to the aftermath of that. It was what he'd always feared and tried to protect Ruby from.

In his head, he knew exactly what he should have done. He should have introduced Ruby gradually to the world's press. He should have made it clear she was no longer an employee. She was a friend. A family friend.

But his heart hadn't been able to keep the slow pace required. He'd already waited ten years for Ruby. He didn't want to wait for the media to catch up with him. He didn't want to waste a tiny second. But his impatience had probably cost him everything.

This was all his fault. Totally his fault.

He should have spoken to Ruby about this. He should have spoken to his advisors. He should have prepared her, taken his time, treated her with the respect and love that she was due.

He was unworthy of Ruby. He'd failed her completely.

And from the look on her face she thought that too.

'I went to the shops...I went to buy us breakfast,' her words faltered. 'I know that they have everything in the kitchen, but I wanted to get something special—for us.'

Her voice was shaky and her eyes were strangely blank, as if she was disengaged. As if she couldn't really comprehend what was happening in the world around her. His heart twisted in his chest. She'd walked into the city. She'd found out about this on her own.

There were tear trails down her cheeks, glinting in the morning sun. He ignored the advisors in his ears and knelt next to her chair, staring at the computer screen in front of her.

'I'm sorry, Ruby. I should have prepared you for this.'

Her eyes widened in clear disbelief. 'You can prepare people for *this*? For these lies? This complete invasion of privacy?' She shook her head. 'They phoned me. Someone phoned me this morning, wanting an interview—'

'What did you say?' butted in Rufus.

Alex held up his hand to silence him.

She was still shaking her head. 'I hung up. How did they get my number?'

Alex took a deep breath. 'It's not hard, Ruby. They do things like this all the time. You get used to it.'

'You get used to *this*? How?'

He reached out and took her hand. It was icy cold and that shot a little fear into his heart. He could see the hopes and dreams for the way all this should go begin to crumble all around him.

It was her face. The expression on her face. She was devastated. Beyond devastated. And he was the one who'd exposed her to this.

She pulled her hand backwards. 'What about Annabelle, Alex? How will you keep Annabelle from this? Is this the kind of life she'll have? Every teenage kiss, every hand-hold, every party plastered across the press?' She was shaking her head and tears were flowing freely now. 'How on earth will you keep her safe from all this?'

*Safe.* The word struck fear inside. Ruby didn't feel safe. But something else had resonated with him. Even now she was thinking about Annabelle in the future. She was raising the issue of trying to protect his daughter.

'We have rules in Euronia, Ruby. Photographers are not allowed to take unofficial pictures of any members of the royal family. We're strict about these things. They know they have to respect our privacy.'

'Really?' She spun the laptop around to face him again. 'So what happened here, then?'

It was one of the photos from the newspapers. A picture from months ago, when he'd first taken her to the café in front of the casino.

'What happened to respecting your privacy? What happened to respecting *my* privacy. This was when I first got here—how many more private pictures do they have of me, Alex?'

Her breaths were ragged, the pain on her face sending shards through his heart. This was exactly what he hadn't wanted to happen. But these last few days his feelings for Ruby had just started to overwhelm him.

She'd been in his mind and his thoughts for ten years. Having her under his palace roof had taken every single element of his self-control. She'd opened his world again—asked him the right questions, made him question his own thoughts and feelings. She'd influenced his relationship with his daughter. It had improved beyond all recognition.

It was almost as if she'd taught him how to be a parent. How to love every part of Annabelle and, more importantly, how to communicate with a little girl who wouldn't talk to him. Before he'd been confused and felt guilty. Now he took each day as it came. His time devoted to Annabelle was never compromised.

Ruby was still crying, the tears slowly trickling down her cheeks. He reached out and touched her cheek but she flinched.

'I'm not the person they say I am,' she whispered. 'I don't want people to write things like that about me.'

His heart was breaking for her. 'Ruby, I'm sorry. I should never have invited you to the ball. I should have waited. *We* should have waited. If we'd introduced you slowly the press would have been easier. My advisors could have told you how to act, what to say. This is my fault.' He shook his head, 'I just didn't want to wait any longer, Ruby. I wanted you to be part of my world—part of Annabelle's world.'

Right now he couldn't care who else was in the room. Right now he was only interested in Ruby. The pain on her face was tearing him apart. More than anything he wanted her to look at him and tell him that was what she wanted too. To be part of his world. But even though she was looking at him it was as if she'd switched off.

She shook her head. 'But that's just it, Alex. I don't *want* someone to tell me how to act and what to say.' She pressed her hand against her chest. 'What's wrong with just me—Ruby Wetherspoon?'

He took both her hands in his. 'Nothing—nothing at all. We can make this better, Ruby. I promise. *I* can make this better. We can work together. We can find a way to deal with the press. I'll find the photographer who took those pictures of us and he or she will never be allowed in Euronia again. This isn't as bad as you think.'

There was a noise behind him. The tiniest clearing of a throat…the squeak of a shoe. Ruby's eyes darted to the advisors behind him. He winced. He didn't need to turn around to know what the expressions on their faces must look like. He'd heard them talk incessantly since they'd knocked on his bedroom door this morning.

Their solution was simple: Ruby must go. The good name of Euronia must be protected and if the Prince Regent wanted to date then it must be handled by the press team.

He hated this. He hated all of this. For the first time in his life he wished he was free of all this. Free of the responsibility. Free of the ties. He wanted to be free to love the woman he'd loved for the last ten years. He wanted to be free to tell the world that. He didn't need to ask their permission.

'Ruby, talk to me. Tell me what you're thinking. Whatever it is you're worried about—we can fix it. We can make this work. You and I can be together. I love you, Ruby. I'm not going to lose you twice.'

She sucked in a deep breath. It was the first time he'd told her how he really felt about her. But this wasn't the way he'd wanted to do that. Telling someone you loved them should be for sunsets and fireworks—not bright libraries, with three other people listening to every word.

Ruby pushed herself up from the chair and walked over to the window, looking out over the gardens. It was almost as if she hadn't heard his words.

'I need to go, Alex. I need to get away from all this. I can't think straight.' She reached out and touched one of the ornate curtains at the window. 'I need to get away from here. This isn't my place. This isn't my home.' She spun around to face him. 'I need to get away from *you*, Alex.'

It was like a wave of cold water washing over him. She hadn't reacted to his words. She hadn't even acknowledged that he'd said he loved her.

Doubts flooded through him. Maybe he'd been wrong all along. Maybe she didn't feel the same way as he did. Maybe this was her way of letting him down gently.

He felt his professional face fall into place—his Prince Regent face—the one he'd never had to use around Ruby.

'Where will you go?' He couldn't help it, his words were stumbling.

This time her eyes seemed more focused. 'I'd always planned on visiting my mum and dad at Christmas. I'll go now. They're in France. I can get there in a few hours.'

Her shoulders straightened. He watched her suck in another deep breath and look his advisors square in the eyes. She was determined. It was almost as if now she'd made a decision nothing would get in her way. She started to walk forward.

He tried to be rational. He tried to think logically. 'I'll arrange for the jet to take you.'

She gave him the briefest nod and walked straight out of the door. Not a single hesitation or backward glance.

His advisors all started talking at once. But Alex couldn't hear them. All he could focus on was the stillness of Ruby's skirts as she walked along the corridor. The spark and joy he'd felt around her last night had vanished. Even the sway in her steps had been curtailed.

His Princess Ruby was vanishing before his eyes.


She couldn't breathe. An elephant was currently sitting on her chest, squeezing every single breath from her lungs.

Her legs burned as she climbed the stairs and strode along the corridor to her room.

Alex had told her that he loved her.

*Alex had told her that he loved her.*

Her heart should be singing. Instead it felt as if it had been broken in two.

All those conversations. All those questions about whether she was sure, whether she was ready.

The cold, hard truth was that she wasn't. Right now she doubted she ever would be. Waking up to see people she didn't know telling lies about her, people the world over reading and believing those lies, was like being dunked in an icy-cold bath.

Was this what her life would become?

She opened the cupboard and pulled out her suitcase, leaving it open on the bed. She started yanking clothes from their hangers, not bothering to fold anything.

Then she stopped, her fingers coming into contact with some of the more delicate fabrics. Some of the more beautiful designs.

Were these clothes even hers?

Should she even take them?

Confused, she walked into the bathroom and emptied the area around the sink with one sweep of her hand into her toiletries bag.

There was a movement to the side of her eye. She sighed. Alex. She needed some space.

Except it wasn't Alex. It was Annabelle, her eyes wide as she looked at the disarray in the room.

Ruby was shocked. She dropped to her knees and put her hands on Annabelle's shoulders. The little girl's bottom lip was trembling.

'Oh, honey,' she said. 'I'm sorry. But I need to go away for a little while. I need to leave.'

Annabelle shook her head. Her mouth opened and she scowled fiercely.

'No.'

It was one word. It was a tiny word—fuelled by emotion. But it was the biggest step in the world.

She flung her arms around the little girl. She hadn't thought it was possible for her heart to break any more. But she hadn't counted on this.

She cradled the blonde curls in her fingers and whispered in Annabelle's ear. 'I love you, honey. And I'm so proud of you for saying that word. You are such a clever little girl.' She pulled back and held Annabelle's face in her hands. 'That's the best word I've ever heard.'

'No.'

Annabelle said it again, and pointed to the case. There was another movement to the side. This time it *was* Alex. His face was pale.

'Ruby?'

She nodded. 'Yes. She spoke to me.'

She kissed Annabelle on the forehead, then lifted her and handed her to Alex as she continued to pack her case.

Alex was the parent here—not her. It was his job to be by his daughter's side. She doubted she could ever fulfil her professional role again. Loving both Alex and Annabelle had wrecked her perspective. Becoming emotionally attached would make leaving harder for them all. She had to draw a line in the sand.

Alex's face was racked with confusion. 'And you're still going to go?'

She nodded. She had to.

Everything was too much right now. She didn't just love Alex. She loved his little girl too. If she didn't leave now she didn't know how her heart could ever recover.

She jammed the last thing into the case and closed it. Picking it up, she turned to face him.

He was clutching his daughter and shaking his head. 'How can you? How can you go now?'

'Because I have to. Because this is the right thing to do.' She stepped up close to him. 'Because if I stay this will only get worse. You think I didn't see the panic on your advisors' faces? You think I don't know that every single action you take could affect the people in this country—your trade agreements, your business? I'm not so stupid as to want to destroy the country that you've built. I'm not that stupid and I'm not that selfish.'

'But what about us?' He glanced down towards Annabelle, who had cuddled into his chest. 'How can you leave us now?' He was getting angry. He was getting frustrated. 'Don't you have a heart?'

She flinched. But it was exactly what she'd needed to hear. It made it so much easier.

'I left my heart in Paris ten years ago, Alex. You should know.'

And she held up her head and walked out of the room before her shaking legs could stop her.

# CHAPTER TWELVE

IT WAS STRANGE, spending Christmas in France. The weather was unseasonably warm. Ruby was used to Christmases in England, with freezing temperatures and snow.

Her mother appeared at the door. She had a pale cream envelope in her hand. 'This came for you. I had to sign for it.' She turned it over and over in her hands.

Ruby sighed. 'Is it from Alex?'

She stared at her desk. It was already littered with A4 envelopes—some from Alex, and some from his advisors. All full of details on how to deal with 'the situation'. Pages and pages of plans for dealing with the press.

A plan for how often she could be seen. A plan for how much time they could spend together. A plan for when Alex could eventually put an arm around her. Followed by detailed protocols and information on the history of Euronia and Leruna. It was like studying for a university degree all over again. But this wasn't a qualification. This was a plan for a life. *Her* life.

And she just didn't know if she was strong enough.

In amongst the plans were little handwritten cards

from Alex. He'd sent one every day, his pleading words increasing in intensity with each card.

'You'll have to speak to him sooner or later,' her mother said. 'He phones three times a day. I'm beginning to feel like he's part of the family already.'

The words twisted inside her. 'I can't speak to him, Mum, you know that. I need some time.'

Her mother sighed and sat down next to her. 'Why do you need time away from the man and the little girl that you obviously love?'

Ruby was shocked. She'd never used those words to her mother. She hadn't said those words out loud to anyone.

'What? You think I didn't know?' Her mother waved her hand. 'It's been written all over your face from the second you got here. I've never seen you so miserable. It was a few lousy newspaper articles. You know what your dad says—today's news, tomorrow's chip paper.' She gave a half-shrug. 'You only made two lines today in the British press.'

Ruby gave a half-smile. Her father had been surprisingly good-natured.

She stared at the letter. 'I don't think I can read anything else from Alex.'

Her mother shook her head. 'It's not from Alex. It's from Leruna. Who would be writing to you from there?'

Her skin prickled. She couldn't have—could she?

She took the heavy envelope in her hand and opened it, sliding the paper out. There was no doubt.

The royal mark was in the top corner. Queen Isabelle.

She blinked. 'Give me a minute, Mum, will you please?'

Her mother nodded and disappeared out through the door. Ruby unfolded the letter on her desk. No typing. This letter was full of beautifully crafted handwriting.

*Dear Ruby*

*I hope this letter finds you well. It was a pleasure to meet you at the Ball and I was delighted to see your obvious affection for Annabelle and your commitment to her.*

*I understand that you are upset over the recent media coverage. Please be assured that this is a cross we all have to bear. I only hope that a little time will give you the strength and courage of your convictions to fight for the love and family that you deserve.*

*Alex and Annabelle have blossomed in these last few months. I have no doubt who is responsible for the transformation of their relationship. The press can be cruel to us all, but I hope that you won't allow others to impact on the life you could have.*

*My granddaughter misses you terribly. The sparkle that had returned to her eyes has gone again.*

*My beloved Sophia is gone. She was a kind-hearted girl with a much wilder spirit than she was credited for. I believe that she would have wanted both Alex and Annabelle to be loved with the passion that they deserve.*

*I want you to know that you will always be welcome as my guest in Leruna. You have our full support.*

*Good grace and wishes,*

*Her Majesty Isabella DeGrundall, Queen of Leruna*

Ruby's head was swimming. She could never have expected this. It wasn't even the words that Queen Isabella had used. It was all the unwritten things in between. She was giving Ruby her blessing. She was acknowledging her presence in Alex and Annabelle's life. The invitation was clear.

'Ruby?'

Her mother was hovering around the door again.

'The car that brought the letter…it's still there. It's waiting for you.'

'Waiting for me?' She glanced outside.

Her mother smiled. 'It seems there's a celebration for New Year's Eve tonight in Euronia.' There was a rustle and she held up a clothes hanger and a shimmering dress. 'Apparently your attendance is non-negotiable.'

The flight took less than an hour. The stewardess helped Ruby into the dress and escorted her down to the waiting car.

Her eyes were squeezed shut for most of the drive as her stomach turned over and over.

So many thoughts and questions spun around in her brain. Although having some space had served her well, reading over the plans for her gradual romance had been mind-boggling.

She didn't want to live her life to a plan. But rational thoughts were starting to creep in. She loved Alex. She loved Annabelle. They weren't your average family. And if Ruby wanted this life she was going to have to work for it.

Was it really so unreasonable for her to learn how to handle the press? Would learning about a new country and its customs really be so different from gaining the professional degree and qualifications she already had?

She knew she had the ability to learn. She knew she had the ability to adapt to different situations—she'd been doing it for years in the health service.

She was thinking with her heart instead of her head. If she thought with her head this all seemed rational—practical. It seemed like something she could actually do.

The car turned down the driveway towards the palace and she gasped. The pink palace was outlined in dozens of white lights. It was spectacular. People from the city were within the grounds. It seemed the party had already started.

The car pulled up in front of the palace doors

and a guard opened the door and held out a hand to help her out.

She glanced at her watch. Eleven o'clock on New Year's Eve. Eleven years ago she'd been in Paris. Eleven years ago she'd met Alex for the first time. Eleven years ago they'd shared their first kiss.

*Alex.* He was standing at the top of the steps waiting for her.

She'd thought she'd hesitate when she saw him again—she'd thought she'd waver.

But she didn't. She moved away from the car and took her first step towards him.

Her dress was shimmering silver, crying out to be touched, but he kept his hands firmly at his sides as she climbed the steps towards him.

The designer who'd made it had assured him it would look perfect on her. But 'perfect' wasn't close enough to how it actually looked.

The silver beads sparkled in the white lights around the palace. If Annabelle were watching she'd think that Ruby was some kind of fairy. It was almost as if a movie spotlight were shining on her.

She stopped just a few steps away, her hair curled around one shoulder, brown eyes fixed on his and her red lips inviting his kiss.

He held out his hand towards her. 'I'm so glad you came, Ruby. I was worried you would never come back to Euronia.'

'I wasn't sure if I wanted to.'

He could see the uncertainty on her face. She still hadn't decided what she wanted to do. This was it. This was his final chance to convince her to stay.

'I don't want to be part of someone's plan, Alex. I appreciate the work that your staff has done. But I don't think I can live my life like that.' She gave a sorry smile and a little shake of her head. 'I can't wait to love you, Alex. I can't wait to love Annabelle. But I don't have royal blood. I haven't been brought up in the same circumstances as you.' She held out her hands. 'I think we both need to face facts. I just don't fit in around here.'

Her dress shimmered some more, reflecting light back up onto her face. She'd never looked so beautiful. She'd never looked so radiant. And he couldn't bear not to touch her for a second longer. His heart was filling with joy and breaking at the same time. She'd told him that she couldn't wait to love him. She couldn't wait to love Annabelle. But it was too hard. There were a million obstacles in their way.

But all that mattered to Alex was the fact that Ruby loved him and his daughter just as much as they loved her.

At the end of the day, what more did he need?

He would do anything to make this work.

He wrapped his arms around her waist and pulled her close.

'Eleven years ago in Paris I met the woman of my dreams. Eleven years ago I met the woman I was destined to be with for ever. Fate tried to get in the way. Life tried to get in the way. But from the first time I met you—from the first time I kissed you—I knew, Ruby. I just *knew*. I think that you did too.'

The palms of her hands were resting against his chest. Her bottom lip was trembling.

He smiled at her. 'Ruby, I don't ever want to let you go. You are the only woman I want by my side. But more than anything I want you to be happy. You are the best woman I've ever known. I love you, Ruby. Annabelle loves you too. I'd love to tell you I don't care what the media says—but that wouldn't be true.'

She flinched and he pressed on, moving one hand from her waist and pressing it above her heart.

'I care because *you* care. I don't want anyone to hurt you. I don't want anyone to upset you. I want you to be happy. I want you to be safe. I want to love you, cherish you and keep you for ever. I want you by my side whatever I do.'

'But what about me, Alex? What about my work? I'm not a stay-at-home kind of girl.'

Even as she said the words she wondered how true they were. She'd already been thinking of changing her role at work and trying to find a less stressful kind of job. She loved her patients. She just didn't love the bureaucracy.

He smiled. 'I want what you want. I want to support you in any work you want to do. What is it you want to do, Ruby? Can you do it Euronia?'

She nodded slowly. 'I want to work with people, Alex.'

'Then you can. We have a hospital here. You can be the people's Princess Ruby. If you want to work there—you can.'

'Really?' Things were starting to seem more real. More possible. More within her grasp.

'I want you to be the person I turn to when I need guidance. I want you to be the person Annabelle comes to when she cuts her knee, quarrels with her friends and...' he grimaced '...needs boyfriend advice. I want you to be the person holding my hand and squeezing it when Annabelle says her first sentence. When she starts school. When she's crowned Queen of Leruna.'

Her voice trembled. 'That's a whole lot of wants, Alex. Some parts even sounded like wedding vows.'

He nodded slowly. 'They did—didn't they?' He reached up and tangled his fingers in her hair. 'Here's another one, then. I *want* to make this work. I want to make this work for you and me.'

Tears were forming in her eyes. 'I want this to work too, Alex. I've missed you, and I've missed Annabelle these last few days. I felt as if I'd left part of me behind. But I still want to be normal too, Alex. I'll let you down. I'm not cut out for this kind of life. I'm just Ruby Wetherspoon from Lewisham.' She gave the slightest shake of her head. 'I can't be Princess Ruby.'

One tear slid down her cheek. He pulled her

closer and whispered in her ear. 'I think you can. I think you and I can figure this out together. There's no one else for me, Ruby. It's just you. Tonight is our anniversary. Tonight, eleven years ago, someone was smiling down from up above and telling me to reach into the crowd and pull the girl in the red coat up next to me. And that was it.'

He pulled back and pressed his hand over his heart.

'That was it for me, Ruby. Our defining moment. Everything in between has been just smoke and mirrors. Everything that's happened has brought us to here and now.' He held out his hand over the palace grounds. 'This is where we're supposed to be right now. This is what we're supposed to be doing.'

'Paris was a fairytale, Alex. Every girl knows that fairytales don't come true.'

He smiled and slipped an arm around her shoulders, turning her to look out over the crowds. 'But fairytales are magic, Ruby—don't you know that? Every girl doesn't get a prince. Just like every guy doesn't get a princess. But I'm hoping that tonight my fairytale comes true.'

The fireworks started immediately.

The crowd in the gardens all turned towards them. They were spectacular. White and gold Catherine wheels streaking across the black sky. Flashes of blue and red confetti cannons. Roman candles and rockets firing into the sky and exploding in a cascade of brilliant lights. The effects were daz-zling.

Multi-coloured waterfall fireworks came at the end of the display, mirroring the fireworks in Paris eleven years ago. They'd been put there at Alex's special request. Would Ruby remember them?

Of course she did. She turned and smiled at him.

'It's almost identical.' Her voice was low and hoarse. 'I haven't watched a firework display since then, Alex. I didn't want anything to spoil the mem-ories I had of Paris.'

His heart lifted. She felt the same as he did. 'Ruby, I love you. I want you to stay with me in Euronia. I don't want you to be Annabelle's speech therapist. I don't want you to be an employee. I don't want you to be waiting in the wings. I'm ready, Ruby. I'm ready to tell the world that I love you and I want you by my side.'

He held his hand up to the fireworks.

'This is for us, Ruby, and I'll recreate these fire-works every year for us. Eleven years ago was the start. I wish we'd had a chance to continue from there. And while I wish my friend Sophia hadn't died I couldn't ever wish my daughter Annabelle wasn't here. Maybe it was always destined that our two countries would be united. But what I know in my heart is that I was always destined for you.'

He knelt down on one knee and pulled the ring he'd had made out of his pocket.

'I love you, Ruby Wetherspoon. Will you do me

the honour of agreeing to become my wife? I promise to love and cherish you for ever. I promise to be by your side no matter what happens. Whatever you want to do, you will have my full support. And I hope I will have yours. What do you think, Ruby? Can we create our own fairytale here, in Euronia?'

The fireworks continued to explode behind her. The shimmering silver dress reflected every one of them in the dark night. The colours lit up Ruby's face and there it was—the sparkle in her eyes again. The thing he'd longed for and hoped to see for the last two weeks.

She reached down and pulled him up. She was smiling. 'Don't kneel for me, Alex. That's not where I want you.' She slipped the custom-made ruby and diamond ring on to her finger. 'I want you right by my side.'

He slipped his arms around her. 'Is that a yes?'

She slid her arms around his neck and tipped her lips towards his. 'That's definitely a yes.'

And he kissed her as the fireworks lit up the sky behind them.

Princess Ruby was here to stay.

# EPILOGUE

RUBY ADJUSTED HER veil nervously while Polly fussed around her.

'How long *is* this train?'

They were currently all enveloped in the back of the car by mounds and mounds of jewelled pale cream satin. She practically couldn't even see her father at this point.

'Twenty-five feet.' She smiled, even though she was afraid to move. 'Apparently it's a tradition.'

'It's a tradition, all right. Can you even walk with this thing?'

Ruby nodded. 'I've been practising.'

Polly's eyes widened. 'You have? When?'

She smiled again. 'At night. Rufus—Alex's private secretary—has helped me for the last few nights. We've practised up and down the main staircase and out through the main doors.'

'Wow.' Polly handed Ruby her red flowers and lifted her hands to straighten the ruby and diamond tiara on Ruby's head. 'Seems like someone has introduced a few traditions of their own.'

'Ooby—look!' Annabelle was practically standing on one of the other seats, waving at the crowds as they passed, her short red bridesmaid dress bouncing around her.

Ruby stretched over. 'Come here.' She gave Annabelle a hug. 'You look beautiful, Annabelle. You're going to be the most gorgeous girl anyone has ever seen.'

The little girl couldn't stop smiling. Her speech was improving every day. Simple words...

The car pulled up outside the church and Ruby couldn't wipe the smile from her face. *This was it.*

It seemed to take for ever for Polly and her father to unwind her dress and the train from the car. Then there was a nod as Polly took Annabelle's hand and led her ahead.

She waved to the crowds and headed to the church door, the heavy train hampering her steps. If she had her way she'd be running down the aisle to meet Alex.

The crowd in the church was hushed. Queen Isabelle turned from the front pew and gave her the tiniest nod of her head. But Ruby's eyes were fixed on Alex.

There was no tradition here. Her groom would never stand facing the front, waiting for her to appear.

Alex had turned around to face her, his bright blue eyes fixed firmly on hers, smiling from ear to ear. He'd never looked more handsome. She'd never been so sure.

Ruby's father took her arm. 'Ready?'

She nodded. 'Always,' she said, and took the first steps that would start her new life.

\* \* \* \* \*

# COMING NEXT MONTH FROM

**HARLEQUIN**

*Romance*

### Available February 3, 2015

## #4459 HER BROODING ITALIAN BOSS
### by Susan Meier
Pregnant and broke, Laura Beth takes a job with brooding yet brilliant artist Antonio Bartulocci. But this fiery Italian proves to be a difficult boss! Can she remind him of all that's good in this life?

## #4460 THE HEIRESS'S SECRET BABY
### by Jessica Gilmore
When heiress and CEO Polly Rafferty discovers her no-strings summer fling had *very* unexpected consequences, her gorgeous new vice CEO, Gabe Beaufils, is the only person she can trust with her baby secret...

## #4461 A PREGNANCY, A PARTY & A PROPOSAL
### by Teresa Carpenter
Falling pregnant after a fling with infamous Ray Donovan was not part of event coordinator Lauren Randall's plan! But can she stop herself from falling for her baby's father?

## #4462 BEST FRIEND TO WIFE AND MOTHER?
### by Caroline Anderson
After a near-miss down the aisle, Amy Driver is rescued by TV chef and best friend Leo Zaccharelli. But after spending time with him and his adorable daughter, Ella, could their friendship lead to forever?

---

HRLPCNM0115

# LARGER-PRINT BOOKS!
## GET 2 FREE LARGER-PRINT NOVELS PLUS
# 2 FREE GIFTS!

### ❦ HARLEQUIN®

*Romance*

*From the Heart, For the Heart*

**YES!** Please send me 2 FREE LARGER-PRINT Harlequin® Romance novels and my 2 FREE gifts (gifts are worth about $10). After receiving them, if I don't wish to receive any more books, I can return the shipping statement marked "cancel." If I don't cancel, I will receive 4 brand-new novels every month and be billed just $4.84 per book in the U.S. or $5.24 per book in Canada. That's a savings of at least 19% off the cover price! It's quite a bargain! Shipping and handling is just 50¢ per book in the U.S. and 75¢ per book in Canada.* I understand that accepting the 2 free books and gifts places me under no obligation to buy anything. I can always return a shipment and cancel at any time. Even if I never buy another book, the two free books and gifts are mine to keep forever.

119/319 HDN F43Y

| | | |
|---|---|---|
| Name | (PLEASE PRINT) | |
| Address | | Apt. # |
| City | State/Prov. | Zip/Postal Code |

Signature (if under 18, a parent or guardian must sign)

### Mail to the **Harlequin®** Reader Service:
**IN U.S.A.:** P.O. Box 1867, Buffalo, NY 14240-1867
**IN CANADA:** P.O. Box 609, Fort Erie, Ontario L2A 5X3
**Want to try two free books from another line?**
Call 1-800-873-8635 or visit www.ReaderService.com.

* Terms and prices subject to change without notice. Prices do not include applicable taxes. Sales tax applicable in N.Y. Canadian residents will be charged applicable taxes. Offer not valid in Quebec. This offer is limited to one order per household. Not valid for current subscribers to Harlequin Romance Larger-Print books. All orders subject to credit approval. Credit or debit balances in a customer's account(s) may be offset by any other outstanding balance owed by or to the customer. Please allow 4 to 6 weeks for delivery. Offer available while quantities last.

**Your Privacy**—The Harlequin® Reader Service is committed to protecting your privacy. Our Privacy Policy is available online at www.ReaderService.com or upon request from the Harlequin Reader Service.

We make a portion of our mailing list available to reputable third parties that offer products we believe may interest you. If you prefer that we not exchange your name with third parties, or if you wish to clarify or modify your communication preferences, please visit us at www.ReaderService.com/consumerchoice or write to us at Harlequin Reader Service Preference Service, P.O. Box 9062, Buffalo, NY 14269. Include your complete name and address.

HRLP13R

## SPECIAL EXCERPT FROM

 **HARLEQUIN**
TM

*Romance*

*Read on for a sneak preview of Jessica Gilmore's
exciting new title,*

### THE HEIRESS'S SECRET BABY

RESOLUTELY POLLY HELD the glass up over the man's face
and tipped it. For one long moment she held it still so that the
water was perfectly balanced right at the rim, clear drops so
very close to spilling over the thin edge.

And then she allowed her hand to move the glass over the
tipping point, a perfect stream of cold water falling like rain
onto the peacefully slumbering face below.

Polly didn't quite know what to expect; anger, shock,
contrition or even no reaction at all. He was so very deeply
asleep after all. But what she didn't expect was for one red-
rimmed eye to lazily open, for a smile to play around the
disturbingly well-cut mouth or for a hand to shoot out and
grab her wrist.

Caught by surprise, she stumbled forward, falling against
the chaise as the hand snuck around her waist, pulling her
down, pulling her close.

*"Bonjour, chérie."* His voice was low, gravelly with
sleep and deeply, unmistakably French. "If you wanted me
to wake up you only had to ask."

It was the shock, that was all. Otherwise she would have
moved, called for help, disentangled herself from the strong
arm anchoring her firmly against the bare chest. And she
would never, *ever* have allowed his other hand to slip around

her neck in an oddly sweet caress while he angled his mouth toward hers—she would have moved away long before the hard mouth claimed hers in a distinctly unsleepy way.

It was definitely the shock keeping her paralyzed under his touch—and she was definitely *not* leaning into the kiss, opening herself up to the pressure of his mouth on hers, the touch of his hand moving up her back, slipping round her rib cage, brushing against the swell of her breast.

Hang on, his hand was where?

Polly pulled away, jumping up off the chaise, resisting the urge to scrub the kiss off her tingling mouth.

Or to lean back down and let him claim her again.

"What do you think you're doing?"

"Saying *au revoir* of course." He had shifted position and was leaning against the back of the chaise, his eyes skimming every inch of her until she wanted to wrap her arms around her torso, shielding herself from his insolent gaze.

*"Au revoir?"* Was she going mad? Where were the panicked apologies and the scuttling out of her office?

"Of course." He raised an eyebrow. "As you are dressed to leave I thought you were saying goodbye. But if it was more of a good morning—" the smile widened "—even better."

"I am not saying *au revoir* or good morning or anything but *what on earth are you doing in my office and where are your clothes?"*

*Don't miss this sparkling new romance by Jessica Gilmore, THE HEIRESS'S SECRET BABY!*

*Available February 2015 wherever Harlequin®
Romance books and ebooks are sold!*

www.Harlequin.com